UNCLE HENRY'S LAST STAND

UNCLE HENRY'S LAST STAND

Alasdair McKee

Richard Drew Publishing
GLASGOW

First published 1989 by Chatto & Windus Ltd.

This edition first published 1990 by
Richard Drew Publishing Ltd.
6 Clairmont Gardens
Glasgow G3 7LW

The publisher acknowledges the financial assistance of the
Scottish Arts Council in the publication of this book

British Library Cataloguing in Publication Data
McKee, Alasdair
    Uncle Henry's last stand.
    I. Title
823'.914 [F]

ISBN 0-86267-278-3

Printed and bound in Great Britain by
Cox & Wyman Ltd., Reading

Contents

Introduction

This is a story of Death, Misanthropy and Apocalypse. In spite of this it is not entirely comic.

It is set in the weeks preceding Armageddon, which is to take the form of a third world war. I will make it perfectly clear here, at the beginning, that it is not my intention to bore the reader with complex 'scenarios' or 'projections' of how such a 'conflict' might arise. I shall leave that to the imagination, although a quick look around at one's leaders and neighbours should not make it too hard to picture. No, rather than relating some grand epic of the apocalypse I wish to tell a simpler and more personal story, in which the end of the world has a small, but not unimportant, part to play.

one

In which the end is nigh

It is a sad and frightened world that doubts the sound of thunder. Especially on a day as close as this, when the afternoon hangs like a fever on every brow and the air is thick enough to be carved up into greenhouses. And yet, at the sound of the first crack and rumble the whole of Princes Street faltered with almost comic choreography. Many stopped dead in their tracks to stare upwards, others feigned calmness and only glanced up and around. The atmosphere grew thicker and thicker until the first big, soft drops began to fall. One, then two, then rain. And with the breaking of the storm came an almost audible sigh of relief as the street once more thawed into activity and all continued to ignore what was so surely coming.

The significance of that episode, three weeks after my tenth birthday, escaped me at the time. But I do know that it was a Friday afternoon, the half day at the end of the summer term – I'm sure that's the only reason that I remember it at all. Not only had we just been released from a year of school, but also from the more immediate torture of that morning's Kirk service, a sadistic injection of spiritual solemnity into the most delirious day of the year. I had often attempted to escape from this service, most recently by pleading family atheism (quite true) and the fact that I was entirely unchristened (another uncharacteristically factual excuse) and thus not worthy to enter a church. It was all to no avail. This argument was not only ignored, but positively nullified by the school chaplain, who unexpectedly baptised me from behind by means of a laying on of hands so vigorous that it induced a mild concussion. However, even this firm blow to the head was not enough to unseat the reasonably tolerant (if at times irreverent) scepticism with which my upbringing had infused my brain. It did mean that I had to spend what seemed like a week or two perched on a bum-numbing pew surrounded by almost frightening Presbyterian austerity, listening to the sort of praise that I imagined God accepting in the same way that I dutifully tolerated being kissed by aunts. Then, at last, it was all over. After surviving another year in an old and respected Scottish school, where Calvinistic atonement for original sin played a large part in the structuring of the curriculum, and was the *raison d'être* of the P.E. department, we were finally free.

At the tail of a tussle of schoolboys I headed down the hill into town, summer seemingly stretching out forever in front of me. But not everybody saw it that way. In fact, when the storm broke that afternoon, only those as young as myself seemed at all annoyed by the sight of rain. Everyone else appeared greatly relieved, if not delighted. We looked around, puzzled and annoyed by the stupidity of these adults. Even at that young age we should have realised just how serious things must have been. For we had seen the Scottish public smile. At the *rain*.

They would not smile for long. Even the impending end of the world could not nudge the weather from its time-honoured position of chief moaning topic. Several reasons could be found for this. There was a comfort to be had in discussing everyday matters like the weather at the expense of darker and perhaps more pressing issues. The subject of the war was skated around with great care in much the same way that we schoolboys would sidetrack a teacher by showing remarkable interest in whatever he had just been saying, in the hope that the bell would ring before the call was made for the handing in of non-existent homework. Admittedly, not everyone averted their gaze from approaching doom. There were

8

those of a more philosophical and dramatic bent who, no doubt frustrated by the lack of an audience for their forthcoming early demise, would rail at those around them 'Fools, can't you see what's happening' etc. I suppose that most people were wilfully ignoring the inevitable, but I'm not sure that it was entirely deliberate. The fact is that it made more sense to talk about the weather. It fitted in. The four horsemen of the Apocalypse would have looked quite ridiculous at a bus stop. Armageddon just didn't belong to the everyday world, it didn't mix well. As an idea in itself it was fine. As a personal nightmare it excelled. But in the supermarket queues it was as if you could see the strings. It was rather like the science fiction B-movies which I enjoyed so much at that age. The foulest alien monsters looked splendid whilst wrestling in mid-ocean or stomping merrily across some cardboard metropolis, but when they came face to superimposed face with the flesh and blood hero (no doubt yelling 'Fools, can't you see what's happening') then it became hilariously clear that some Czech émigré special effects wizard had his hand planted firmly up their backsides. And in the streets and buses, shops and bars of the city, amongst so many ordinary flesh and blood faces, that was just how the Apocalypse appeared – absurd by contrast.

Which is why, within a few minutes of the storm breaking, the conversation had returned to moaning about the weather. Besides, there were other, more obvious reasons why the weather still reigned supreme. It could be argued that, although hackneyed, 'Cold for the time of year, isn't it?' somehow has the edge as a conversation opener over 'Good morning, we're all going to die.'

I doubt if that phrase was on the lips of any of the faces that now faded back from the windows, back to their counters and desks. I watched them from the Gardens, sheltering beneath a broad horse-chestnut, eating the first ice cream of summer freedom and still puzzled by these crazy adults who laughed at the play-stifling rain as they went about their business. If the peculiar normality of the situation was to change, if mass panic or anger were to break out, then I would not be around to see it happen. I would be elsewhere, for, before their world could end, the backside was to drop out of mine.

two

In which I display sheer carelessness

The paths of my mother and myself crossed only briefly. Within fifty minutes of safely delivering me into daylight she decided that this world was not big enough for both of us (I had been a large, late and generally awkward baby) and promptly died. I was never entirely sure why she did this but, given my extreme lack of years (or hours), I think I may safely assume that it wasn't something I had said. Thus assured, my childhood was spared the burden of guilt in which so many semi-orphans are inclined to indulge. The only burden was to be my father's, for he was now left with the task of single-handedly bringing up a child – as well as saving the world.

I am not sure how long it was before my father, with his pathological appetite for overwork, realised that his wife had died and that a son and heir had just entered his life. It might have been days for all I know, for I seldom saw him at home once I was old enough to be aware of his absence. It was not that he avoided coming home, more that he engaged in his working life with an almost crusading fervour and thus often forgot about trivial matters like eating and sleeping. The unlikely profession to which this humanitarian passion applied itself was ophthalmic optics. Having been, in his youth, financially frustrated in his ambition to train for one of the more esoteric branches of high medicine, he had embarked upon a career in the 'caring' profession whose training was within his means.

This forced detour did not dampen his enthusiasm in the least. He regarded sight as one of our most precious gifts and spent every available hour working, with what remained of the Health Service, to restore full vision to the old, poor and unfortunate who lived in the precincts of his dockland practice. And their health was not his only concern. I am sure that in his own idealistic way he felt that the lifting of this veil of myopia from so many downtrodden eyeballs might enable them to see more clearly the injustices perpetrated against them – to look beyond to some promised land. And so this retinascope radical slaved away in the darkness of his test room, emerging occasionally to blink like a pit pony at the daylight and the rapidly growing son that had been left in his hands.

Despite my mother's inconsiderate demise, my father was not particularly worried about the prospect of looking after either himself or me. He was a liberated sort, and proud of it, who would quote such favourite mottoes as – 'The man who doesn't know how to cook for himself deserves to starve' – and would often tell of how even the toughest old salts of sailors were incredibly adept at darning their own socks. However, from what I can remember of my father's cooking, any man who does cook for himself, and others, like that, deserves to *hang*, let alone starve. His personal philosophy was about as efficacious in the kitchen as his grander humanitarian principles had been in changing the world at large. Fried potato, as far as I recall, played a major part in my father's cooking. Fried potato and enormous steaming broths of unbeliev-able consistency whose solidity was an almost alchemical reversal of the principle of the stock cube – turning ordinary liquid stock into solid blocks of soup. I am surprised that my mind and stomach were not scarred for life although, to this day, despite all the events of my childhood, the deaths, the loneliness, the war, I still have occasional nightmares about fried potato.

In spite of his culinary incompetence I rather enjoyed being brought up by my father. Admittedly I didn't see a lot of him as he worked most of the hours that God (as in tolerant scepticism) gave

11

him. However, on the rare occasions when he wasn't working, like Sundays, I would invariably have my father's undivided attention as he seldom went out anywhere. Although he was prepared to embrace the whole of humanity in his own philanthropic way, he seemed quite happy to leave its individual members well alone at weekends. He had few friends – I sometimes wonder if he wasn't in fact quite lonely – but whatever the reason it suited me perfectly at the time, as it meant endless games and trips to the park and hills. At other times, before school age, I was often looked after by kindly neighbours, who would keep an eye on me as I grubbed about in the garden, and who first introduced me to real food.

At the age of five I was sent off to school, not near home but just along the road from the practice. This allowed me to be picked up between tests and left to amuse myself with a rubber stamp and any other interesting bits and pieces thrown up by the shelves and cupboards of the basement. His patients grew used to the sight of my father dashing in and out of the practice, and not only to pick up me. Not satisfied with merely saving the sight of some fragile old soul he would then insist on running her home in the car and would arrive back to catch his breath before ushering the next patient into the test room, whose cool darkness allowed it to act as work place, advice bureau and confessional.

It was also able to provide a great deal of entertainment for me. At the end of the working day I would sometimes be allowed in for a real, or more often comic, eye test. With all the lights extinguished, and me dwarfed by the huge adjustable chair, Father would run cackling about the room, threatening the vilest tortures (tickling) while I was reduced to helpless giggles. He would get me to read the anagrammatic pyramid of the sight chart which he swore had been read in distinct syllables by an elderly Polish gentleman who, after smiling cautiously, had remarked that he thought the joke a little risqué for such a public place.

On other occasions I would act as guinea pig, whenever some new piece of equipment arrived. The latest acquisition had been some device which tested for glaucoma by measuring the internal pressure of the eye, or something like that. Whatever it did I wasn't too impressed. Father declared it as an absolute wonder – utterly invaluable. 'Come come,' he cried, 'surely you want to do your bit for modern medicine. After all, we don't want all these geriatrics rampaging around with exploding eyeballs, do we?' I agreed that this was to be avoided at all costs, but did he have to try it out on me? Yes, he did.

As I grew towards my tenth birthday I became prematurely independent. I was old enough to return home from school alone, sometimes to the care of neighbours, but mostly to fend for myself. I was happy enough to sit in our cluttered house, reading or watching television (of which father didn't really approve) until he arrived home. He began to arrive home later and later as time expanded to permit the already ridiculous work load he had taken upon himself. Now that I was a little older, and especially now that I was in the practice far less often, I must have seemed slightly less of a responsibility, so father was once more able to take on the world at full steam.

The afternoon of the thunderstorm, the last day of term, I had spent a short time looking around the shops, waiting for the rain to stop. As was now my habit I made my own way home and so was not to witness the events of that afternoon in the practice.

The denizens of the waiting-room were used to Father's rushing about, but they weren't prepared for what they saw that day. The unflappable receptionist had most definitely flapped. Men in uniforms ran in from a siren-echoing street. They emerged several minutes later from the test room, carrying a sheet-covered body on a stretcher to the waiting ambulance. This did not inspire confidence in those who were not entirely sure of the risks involved in this eye-testing business. What kind of an eye doctor goes around killing off his patients? And have you seen the fearsome-looking machines he's got in there? This unfortunate incident, and the speculation which it aroused, would soon be passed round the bush telegraph of shops and tenement doorways. In fact, there is no doubt that the panic it caused could have been enough to completely ruin my father's reputation. Had it not been him under the sheet.

three

In which my fate is uncertain

After the initial numbness, death leaves behind it a strange residue of intense and vivid life, into which the bereaved are suddenly plunged. The mind is purged of all emotion and cleared of all that is mundane. The senses sharpen like an autumn day. In other words, if there is anything to be said for bereavement, inheritance aside, it is that it acts as a most effective spiritual and mental enema. In later life, whenever I have found myself sinking into a trough of tedious routine, I have occasionally tempted fate by thinking almost fondly of times of great sorrow and loss, when at least life took on a certain stimulating intensity. However, at the age of ten I was not overly concerned with escaping from spiritual mediocrity, least of all if it involved the feeling that I was now completely and utterly alone.

It always feels far more noble to protest against injustice if it has been perpetrated against someone else. Then it has less of a ring of sour grapes about it. And so it was that I went about feeling sorry for myself via the unfairness of Father's death as it concerned him. Which of course it did not. But still I protested his cause. He had devoted his life to helping others. He had even cooked for me . . . and it was still a great injustice. And very unfair as well.

Helpless grief mixed with outrage. I believed in God just long

14

enough to hate him. In my mind there danced a vision of me assaulting the mist-shrouded celestial pillars with a sledge hammer. And then I believed again just long enough to pray that He would take care of Father, because if He didn't. . . Then of course, if God did not exist, I would have to find another scapegoat. The rest of the world would do, and became the object of my revenge, which I was not entirely sure how to realise. Until that is, I remembered the war. I was not a great one for the news, but I had gathered one thing. They said there was going to be a war. A war to end all wars, and everything else besides. Good. That would show them.

While I waited for the annihilation of the planet to settle my personal grudge, there still remained the problem of what was to be done with me. On the day that my father's heart decided to give up its unequal struggle I had been waiting at home for his arrival. It grew quite late, but this was not unusual as he often worked late on Fridays. It was only when I heard footsteps on the gravel outside and low voices approaching the door that I began to experience the first sensations of discomfort. The bell rang. I answered the door in my stocking soles to find myself being bundled inside by a figure that I just had time to recognise, by the shapelessly fashionable pinkness of its boiler suit, as Aunt Margaret. 'Aunt' Margaret was not an Aunt at all, but an old friend of my mother's who had spent the last ten years pestering my father over whether he was taking proper care of me. She was far too liberal to suggest that a single man, even my father, was incapable of bringing up a child, but still she managed to commandeer me on several occasions, times which made me long to return home, even to fried potato.

On this particular occasion she was bringing the news. At first I struggled to put a brave face on the whole affair, mostly because I knew that any display of grief would instantly trigger a bout of smothering sympathy from Aunt Margaret, who crouched before me, hands on my shoulders, looking with painful sincerity (she had never liked my father) into my glazed eyes.

My brave face lasted quite well over the last evening that I spent at home. Half stunned and half on the defensive I remained surprisingly calm, even managing to eat a small meal, which Margaret eked with disgust from Father's homely cupboards. It was not until I went to bed that grief finally took over. My only comfort was an old brown bear, who returned from a cupboard-exile imposed by my growing up. He bore no grudges, and gently lulled me to sleep with the warm smell of sawdust and the past. A scent which can still take me back to warmer, safer days.

four

In which my worst fears are realised

I awoke early the next morning. At first it felt like any other morning until the terrible truth began to dawn. I looked across at the clock. The second hand ticked unstoppably round, dragging me further and further away from a time when Father had been alive and everything had been as it should be. It was like finding myself on the wrong train as it pulls away from the platform. Nothing is going to change the fact that it is the wrong train, nor is there any way that it can be turned back, but still the panic grows as the platform recedes. The only difference was that I could not get off at the next stop and start again. Not that I didn't try. I became lost in a world of 'what if' and 'if only', imagining different circumstances with such ferocious desperation that the truth would be momentarily suspended, only to come crashing down even harder than before as soon as reality reared its ugly head.

The ugly head that reality happened to be rearing that morning belonged to Aunt Margaret, and it appeared round the door of my room in the company of a tray laden with toast and a glass of milk. Her unnatural presence in the house brought home even more the strangeness of the situation. And breakfast in bed was another mistake. The prematurely independent child cannot abide pampering and has an almost bottomless capacity for guilt when made the centre of attention. Father and I had worked as a team and I greatly resented falling victim to this kind of mollycoddling. Mind you, at that particular time I would have resented medical attention had I been run over by a bus.

'Did you sleep well?' she asked.

I grunted in a non-committal fashion and drank some milk.

'It's a very nice day. Some fresh air would do you good.' She threw back the curtains and, damn it all, it was a very nice day. The sun streamed in with a vengeance. I cursed it for daring to contradict the blackness of my mood. It is always difficult to accept that the rest of the world is carrying on as per usual despite the shattering importance of one's own personal tragedy. I wanted the world to go away and leave me alone. I *was* alone, and I wanted to be alone by myself. But the world just perched itself on the edge of a clothes-littered chair and benignly watched as I vacantly prodded my toast.

'Come along now, eat up your breakfast and then we can get started.'

'Started on what?' I mumbled, suddenly remembering the bear and trying to hide him under the covers.

Margaret rose from the chair. A vest fell onto her foot. She removed it gingerly.

'I'll leave you to finish your toast and get washed and dressed. Then you can pack what you will need.'

'Pack? Why?' I was not at my most eloquent that morning.

'You can't stay here by yourself,' she laughed. I failed to see the joke. 'You shall be coming to live with Uncle Peter and me. Now hurry along.' She half closed the door behind her.

I was stunned. I sat gaping in horror and would have remained that way for some time had I not dropped a piece of toast marmalade side down on my pyjamas. I peeled it off absent-mindedly and wiped off the marmalade with the napkin that had found its way onto the tray. This was another shock. Where on earth could she have found a napkin in our house?

Surely there had been some mistake. Father would never have left me in her hands. He was always furious when she came round to pester him. Whenever she commented on the running of the house he would lapse into broad Scots vernacular and suggest that she went away and boiled her head. Amongst other things. But here I was, and what could I do? Even Father at his most forceful had been unable to persuade her to leave us alone, so what chance would I have? There would be little use in arguing.

Perhaps I could run away to the circus, as was the tradition. No, I had never liked circuses. Maybe I should find a lawyer. Hire an assassin. Defect. Maybe . . .

'Are you up yet?' the voice tried to balance the kindness required by the situation with the impatience of one who has a pathological mania for tidiness. Aunt Margaret had come to tidy up my life. No chance.

'Are you up yet?' the head appeared round the door. I made a careful survey of the bedclothes which still enveloped me up to the chin and, having weighed up the evidence, replied 'No.'

Margaret parried this with a still patient 'Well do try to hurry a little. I know it isn't easy. But Uncle Peter will be coming to pick us up at eleven.'

It was no use. I knew that I couldn't stay here by myself, so I decided to get up after all. Outside I could hear the sound of other children revelling in the first summer holiday morning. I swore vengeance. On the smaller ones. They sounded as if they were in another world. I was trapped inside a goldfish bowl. I was on another planet, transported there by some evil power. But no. I was in my bedroom and Father was dead. And I was going to live with *her*.

I cheered myself up by remembering that the world could end at any moment. Maybe I could last out in here until it did. That plan was another non-starter. I needed to go to the toilet. I shuffled across the landing to the bathroom. Only *my* toothbrush remained, along with a bar of soap and just one towel. No shaving-brush, no razor, no glass that held the two false front teeth lost in Father's rugby-playing days, the ones he would take out to impersonate vampires. Everything had gone. Margaret was wasting no time in starting the great tidy-up. I think that part of the plan was to remove any obvious reminders of Father, and thus avoid upsetting

19

me any further. Some hope. Their absence glared obviously from the empty shelf much as the lack of Father filled every room with an almost tangible emptiness. I just wanted to hide and wait for everything to end. Nonetheless I gave myself a cursory wash and shuffled back across the landing.

'Good boy,' said the voice of reason from below. 'Now get yourself dressed and pack up what you will need. Bring enough clothes and any games or books that you might want.'

I pulled on some clothes and set about stuffing others into a suitcase. I packed enough of everything to last until the end of the world (sometime before next Thursday if it was to fit in with my underwear supplies) and added several books, a pack of cards and a few games that I could play by myself. Carefully concealed beneath a pullover lurked the bear. I didn't want to take much else as that would be an admission to myself that this was more than just a temporary measure. I would be back soon. Wouldn't I?

At the appointed hour Uncle Peter arrived in his big, red estate car. He greeted me cheerily but I didn't mind too much. I quite liked Uncle Peter as he could be funny sometimes, and I was sure that he must have married Margaret while she was still human. I was allowed to sit in the front as we drove across town. Peter made pleasant conversation, asked me about school and sport and generally did his best at trying to communicate with a shell-shocked sullen child. I grunted politely in reply and tried to ignore Margaret's interjections from the back.

'I hope you remembered to bring your toothbrush, comb, socks, towel, shoes . . .'

'Kitchen sink,' interrupted Peter in an attempt to lighten my load.

'Peter!' Margaret snapped quietly. 'This is no time for sarcasm. We want Roderick to feel at home, don't we?'

Of course she did. Just so long as I was brushed, scrubbed and boiled before entering the pristine splendour of her Georgian New Town flat. I had been there before of course, and I was quite sure, and fairly determined, that I would most definitely not feel at home. How could I in such a place, decorated in determined modern style with furniture that consisted entirely of corners, making comfort impossible. But comfort was not of the essence. This flat was the design-child of the marriage of minds between a fashionable architect (Peter), and an aunt (Margaret). There was no other way it *could* look.

I was shown to the spare bedroom which was white and stark with a blue roller-blind on the window and a framed poster on the wall which said something in French under a picture of a not particularly attractive building.

'Unpack some of your things,' said Margaret, 'and then we can have some lunch.'

A shiver ran up my spine. Father may have lacked culinary expertise, but to compensate for this he was blessed with a complete lack of imagination, so that you always knew what you were going to find on your plate, and better the enemy that you know. . . This could not be said of Margaret. Everything she cooked arrived at the table incognito. To her originality was all. Like the furniture, it was the effect that counted. Taste didn't get a look in. A meal was to be judged by its ingenuity, a fruit by its obscurity. Fortunately for me the approach of the war had severely curtailed foreign trade, so Margaret was rather more limited than usual in her choice of ammunition for the assault on my simple and unsuspecting palate. That first meal was relatively innocuous, as she had just done something to some cheese, and I thanked my lucky stars that I had not been forced to relive my last encounter with Margaret's cooking. Mind you, in that particular case 'cooking' was hardly the right word, as that meal had been quite raw. Father and I had been invited to a lunch party one weekend. We attended, with the same sense of duty with which we had been invited, to find that the main course was some kind of oriental fish. Raw fish. I remember far less about the fish than I do of Father's sea-lion impersonation, which was as remarkable for its veracity as for its effect on the company. But now there would be no such humour to lighten life in the flat. And when I discovered that Peter was to be away on business for a week or so, leaving me alone with Margaret, it seemed that there was no hope whatsoever. But then, little did I know that, in the not too distant future, rescue was to come from a most unlikely quarter.

five

In which it appears that things
can only get worse

There was so much stripped wood in Aunt Margaret's kitchen that even the yucca plants looked nervous. Wakening in a strange room had added to my already confused state and, as I was to find for many days to come, the morning ritual of remembering hit hard after the relative comfort of sleep. There was no clock in the bedroom, so I had no idea of what time it was. I barely knew what day it was until the silence of the streets outside suggested that this must be Sunday. Pulling on my dressing-gown I quietly made my way to the kitchen.

Once there, I noted that it was still only quarter past six and everyone else was still asleep. The sun was now above the rooftops of the buildings on the opposite side of the crescent. Fenced in below sat a clump of green, a few small trees and shrubs, in the centre of the ring of houses. It looked quite patronised by their grand fanlights and brass knockers. Everything was quiet. Except my stomach, which cried out for breakfast. A search through the cupboards found a bowl and some breakfast cereal whose undoubted nutritional virtues were scant compensation for the dull reading provided by the box. I much preferred the kind that supplied up to one hundred per cent of the necessary daily intake of plastic dinosaurs, but even this fibrous stuff was edible if drowned in milk.

Once I had eaten, and still hearing no signs of life, I went back to my room and dressed. Then I headed for the door that led out onto the stairs. Down two stone flights I went, then, with a creak, the heavy black front door was open. I had only intended going for a walk but, on encountering fresh air properly for the first time in two days, I suddenly felt tempted to run away somewhere. I almost went back for my suitcase, but found that the front door had locked behind me. I decided against ringing the bell at this hour and instead stepped down onto the pavement and began to walk.

The streets were deserted, the only sounds those of the sparrows that squabbled in the hedges of the public garden at the end of the crescent. A small gate in the metal paling was unlocked, so I pushed it open and went in. I found an old wooden bench, covered in moss, on which was bolted a brass plaque, declaring that someone, now deceased, had loved this place. Bully for them. I took their place and looked around at the Sunday morning emptiness. I wondered if this was what it would be like if they did have a war. Would it be as peaceful as this, with all the people gone? If so, then it was definitely a very good idea. As the sun began to lift the early chill, the gentle quietness of the garden began to calm me down. With time to stop and think I felt almost happy, almost prepared to accept what was happening, to go along with it and make the most of things. I would accept my fate, and sit in this garden in the early morning, away from everyone else. Things would be all right. I settled back in the seat, feeling much better. Then I heard the voice. It shouted 'Hello there!' in that raucous 'I'm home now' way, in that infectiously enthusiastic way. It was Father's voice. And this was Sunday morning. We should be away by now, into the park, or perhaps to the sea. I jumped out of the seat and ran out through the gate, spinning this way and that to look down every street, at every doorway, up at every window, all around at every space that remained so maliciously empty. At first I felt rather foolish as I stood in the middle of the street, and looked furtively around to make sure that no one had seen me. Only the crusty old houses were watching, so I began to smile. Then to laugh. Once I had

23

reached that emotional peak there was only one way to go. I began to cry. The truth had finally come home, the concussion had worn off. There, in the middle of that deserted city, I began to sob.

I navigated my way back through misty eyes, tripping up the high kerb then flopping onto the doorstep. I had given up. I was stuck here, lonely, miserable and in the hands of Aunt Margaret. I would die on her doorstep, just to embarrass her.

But I didn't. I was still sitting there with my head on my knees when she came rushing out an hour later in something of a panic and nearly tripped over me.

'Good Lord. There you are. I nearly broke my neck over you.' I cursed my lack of proper positioning. 'Where have you been? We were worried to death when we found you missing. Where did you go?'

'Nowhere,' I said to my knees.

'What were you doing?'

'Nothing.'

'Well come inside now or you'll catch a chill on that cold step.'

'Don't care.'

This could have gone on indefinitely had a neighbour not appeared. He obviously knew who I was and had the audacity to be understanding. If pleas, threats and cajoling could not shift me, there was one thing that could. At the sound of the first 'Poor little soul' I was up the stairs like a shot.

I did not go back down the stairs for several days. I had no particular desire to go out, and even less to go out with Margaret. She would occasionally 'pop out' to the shops, or briefly visit friends, but mostly she was there, fussing and bothering. I spent a great deal of time in my room, slumped on the bed, reading or just moping. I read *Kidnapped*, which I had picked up almost by mistake from my bookshelf, but soon became engrossed in its tales of intrigue and adventure in the Highlands. It helped to make the time pass a little less slowly.

At the end of the week this routine of hiding in a book in my room, until forced out by meals, was finally broken. Margaret wakened me early that morning.

'I'm afraid you shall have to get up. We are going into town today.' She said. As far as I was concerned we were already in town, but I didn't like to be pedantic.

'What for?' I asked instead.

'Well, we have to go and see your Daddy's solicitor about his will. It's just a formality that has to be cleared up. I think it would be best if you came along too. Besides, some fresh air and exercise will do you good . . .'

I didn't really feel like going anywhere, but there didn't seem to be much choice. Besides, at the back of my mind there still lurked the hope that a lawyer might be able to rescue me from my predicament. This inspired me enough to get dressed and join Margaret for breakfast.

It was another hot, sunny day. If this was to be our last summer then it was certainly making the most of it. We walked along the crescent, up the hill and across Queen Street. Past the BBC offices and round the corner. A brief halt was made on George Street so that Margaret could go to the bank, then we were down amongst the bustle of Princes Street. There was no thunder to still the crowd today and we waded along towards the East End. Although it was busy the town seemed strangely quiet. Even the one o'clock gun had been silenced, supposedly due to technical problems, although everyone knew the real reason. Besides, with the absence of tourists that year it was no great loss to the locals. With no one to jump out of their skins there was little fun to be had in everybody calmly checking their watches. That is, if even the locals could remain calm at the sound of a loud bang. It was still only ten o'clock, three hours to go before nothing happened, as we walked up the Mound towards the Old Town, with its crooked tenements and cool dark closes.

All the way from the flat Margaret had kept up a constant barrage of plans for me. A holiday this summer, perhaps a change of school, trips to their holiday cottage in the Borders. It all sounded dreadful and I let most of it pass over my head. Despite my brief breakdown on Sunday I had returned to sullen, stubborn form, refusing to believe that any of this was going to happen, however strong the evidence. Although I could not picture any real alternative I was sure that something had to turn up. It certainly would, and we were only a matter of yards from it.

We turned into the close, conveniently near the courts of the High Street, where Mr Dougal, the family solicitor, had his offices.

'This shouldn't take long,' said Margaret as we climbed the stairs, 'and then we shall go for some lunch somewhere. Uncle Peter is arriving back this evening and I thought we would go and meet him at the station.'

She pushed open the green door with the brass plaque into a seemingly ancient office. Behind a heavy wooden desk sat a secretary, with a stern face and elderly hooked nose (to go with the rest of her face). She rose as we entered and gave Margaret a dirty look. This cheered me up a bit.

'Mrs Calder. To see Mr Dougal,' Margaret said.

'If you will just take a seat for a minute please.' She disappeared into another room, possibly to waken Mr Dougal, for he stifled a yawn as he emerged and looked a trifle bleary-eyed.

'Hello, hello,' he said warmly, shaking hands with Margaret. 'And you must be young Roderick.' I nodded. 'Very pleased to meet you, and very sorry to hear about your father. There are many who will miss him. He was a good man. Aye, a very good man was your father.'

He stood nodding sage consent at his own remarks, remaining silent for quite some time. I thought he might drop off again, but he started when Margaret cleared her throat and revived from his reverie of respect. The nice thing about him was that he seemed to mean it.

'Yes, well we'll get down to the matter in hand. I think it's best if you wait here for the time being young man. I won't keep your aunt for long.' Sensing perhaps that this was no great loss he winked as he ushered her into the office.

The secretary smiled at me and then returned to her work. I sat back in the green leather chair and looked up at the mouldings on the ceiling with their trailing cobwebs. All this way with Margaret and I had to sit outside. I sighed and picked up a magazine. It contained a lot of pictures of big houses and the people who owned them. There was even a picture of a room very like Margaret's with a man leaning on the mantelpiece. In other words, it was very boring, so I put it back down.

From the other room I could hear the steady drone of Mr Dougal's voice. And then something which didn't sound at all routine. It was Margaret's voice rising into an undignified squawk of 'WHAT?'

The secretary and I started and looked up. She smiled again, then pretended not to listen as one voice remained calm and businesslike while the other shrilled with apparent disbelief, then sounded positively angry. I was, to say the least, intrigued. A long silence followed, then the door opened.

'Thank you for your help Mr Dougal,' said Margaret curtly.

'Not at all. And if there's anything else I can do, don't hesitate to get in touch.' He opened the door for us.

'Your aunt will explain the details to you. Meanwhile, if you should need me, here's my card'. I took it and tucked it carefully into my pocket. He shook hands with both of us and winked again as we left.

This time as we walked through town there was not a sound from Aunt Margaret. Despite my burning curiosity I decided to take advantage of this brief respite and asked no questions, even though I knew that anything that could keep Aunt Margaret quiet just had to be big!

six

In which the truth is revealed

Aunt Margaret's silence was maintained for most of the day. We ate lunch in a basement café, not far from the flat, where she sat nursing her coffee and staring into space. Her only other movements were an occasional shake of the head or tightening of the jaw. Any tentative enquiries on my part were dismissed by remarks that it was all quite routine, just what had been expected. Her version of the routine events of the morning was stated with such firm conviction that I knew she had to be lying.

We returned to the flat where Margaret went about some culinary enterprise with taciturn vigour while I retired once more to my room to amuse myself for the afternoon. As promised, we went off to the station to meet Peter. As we drove through the streets, empty in the early evening hiatus between work and play, Margaret seemed to brighten a little, no doubt at the prospect of some moral support. The station was busy and the train a little late, but before too long we were all back at the flat.

Dinner passed in a pleasantly conversational manner. Peter said that his trip had been very successful and entertained us with a tale of being trapped in a lift with a Japanese conference delegate who spoke little English, and could only talk about the weather, of which there was very little in the lift. He asked what I had been up to and I told him that I had just been reading and playing in my room. The business of the solicitor was not mentioned.

At least not until I had settled myself in the sitting-room to watch a television documentary about the remarkably obnoxious habits of a deceptively innocuous-looking jungle rodent. Margaret and Peter were washing up in the kitchen, and, when the news came on, not wishing to hear how much further we had all slipped down the greasy slope of self-destruction, I switched off the television and ambled over to the kitchen door. I was just about to go in, but stopped when I heard my name mentioned in a rather heated discussion.

'But, if that's what his father wanted then it isn't really up to us to argue about it.'

'Peter. You just don't understand.'

'Maybe not, but I don't see what can be done about it. After all, he is Roderick's only living relative, which is more than we can say. We're not connected at all.'

'That isn't the point.'

'Then what is the point?' Peter sounded exasperated.

'The point is that Henry Dundas in an evil old bastard. You have no idea what he's like.'

'Oh, come on, he can't be all that bad.' Earthenware crockery thudded forcefully onto pine work surface.

'And what do you know about it? Have you ever met him? Well I have. And it's not an experience I ever hope to repeat. The things he says! The man is a self-confessed, no, self-proclaimed mis-anthrope.'

This was a word that intrigued me. Was it anything like lycanthrope?

Margaret railed on. 'You ask anyone who's ever met him. Or any of the poor souls that live in that God-forsaken glen of his. I think Roderick's father's mind must have snapped before his heart did to even think of sending him to stay with that man. Do you know, I have actually heard him say in public that he couldn't wait for them to have this war. He said that he thought the planet could do with "cleaning up". Well I'm not having it. The whole thing is ridiculous. Roderick is going to live with that evil old swine over my dead body!'

Things were definitely looking up. All I had to do was dispose of Margaret then I could go and live with an uncle that I had never heard of before, who was apparently a werewolf. I was beginning to cheer up when Margaret stormed out of the kitchen, wringing her hands in a tea-towel.

'Oh,' she said when she saw me. It was obvious that I must have heard every word, but somehow her conspiracy of silence seemed to balance out morally my eavesdropping, for she failed to show any anger.

'There is something I have to tell you,' she said, and sat me down in a chair. She related the news of what I saw as my imminent release with infinitely more emotion than she had managed for Father's death. I listened carefully and tried not to smile.

As I lay in bed that night, for the first time in a week I was actually looking forward to another day. Very soon my time here would be over. I knew that something would come up, I knew that Father wouldn't really have left me with her. I dozed off with a smile on my face, feeling far happier than I had done for ages. But then, I still had an awful lot to learn about Uncle Henry.

seven

In which I prepare to leave

I was delighted to learn that Uncle Henry did not live in Edinburgh and even more pleased when I found out that his home was set amongst the mountains of the Highlands. I had never been fond of city life, so this seemed like a double boost – escape from Aunt Margaret and the crowded, noisy streets. From the bookcase I pulled a large, flat atlas. I searched the area around Inverness and there, thirty miles or so to the south west, was the village that Margaret had mentioned. It sat in a high glen, or possibly on top of a hill (we had only just started on contours in geography), but the presence of a stream, running down the middle, made a valley more likely. Closer examination revealed, a mile or so up the hillside from the village, a tiny black square, accompanied by the legend 'Halfway House'. That must be it, the house in which Uncle Henry lived. It looked excitingly remote and the location fitted in well with the *Kidnapped* adventures that ran through my head, although I tried not to think about David Balfour's wicked uncle. Mine would never be like that, I assured myself, not if Father had wanted me to go there.

I still knew very little about Uncle Henry. The mysteries of the previous day had unfolded slowly. Margaret had eventually, and grudgingly, parted with all the information she knew about Uncle

31

Henry – or, at least, all that she was prepared to tell me. It transpired that he was in fact a great-uncle of some kind, a younger cousin of my paternal grandfather, although Margaret was unsure of the details and seemed in no mood to dwell upon them. He lived by himself in a house that had long been in the family, had never been married and, other than that, there was little else that Margaret could, or would, tell me about him. She was unsure of his age and gave a physical description which only ran to the fact that he was very tall and had a beard. So, this was all the information that I had about him, apart from that word that I overheard in the kitchen. 'Misanthrope'. I replaced the atlas and looked around for a dictionary. I had been well trained by my father in the use of reference books. If I asked the meaning of any word I was invariably sent off to look it up, a habit which no doubt aided the expansion of my vocabulary no end whilst allowing Father to maintain his air of omniscience even when I came up with a really tricky one. I found the dictionary with some difficulty. It was red. Dictionaries, as everyone knows, are always black, like the sacred Oxford oracle which sat in the cabinet at home. But this was red. Therefore I was sure it must be an impostor. It had a modern feel to it, to match the flat, and this, allied to its colour, immediately made me doubt its veracity. And so, when I discovered that a misanthrope was in fact a hater and distruster of mankind, I decided to take it with a pinch of salt. Then again, even if I had believed it completely, my own grudge against the world meant that I failed to see anything particularly reprehensible in those sentiments. Besides, to be quite honest about it, I was just a bit relieved to discover that he wasn't a werewolf after all.

Even if Uncle Henry had been prone to a bestial full moon metamorphosis I doubt if Margaret could have spoken of him with greater disgust or anger. She spat his name out and endowed the 'uncle' part with a vicious sarcasm which seemed a little hypocritical, considering that he had the far greater claim to such familial titles than she pretended to have. Her behaviour at that time was rather difficult to account for. Either it resulted from a genuine affection for me, and anger at losing me, or else it was due to her obvious dislike of Uncle Henry, perhaps because he was a real relation. Whatever the reason, her attitude was ill-disguised. Whether this was calculated to draw me to the anti-Henry cause, or

32

was just too genuine to hide, I will never know, but it failed to dampen my spirits in the slightest and made me all the more sympathetic towards Uncle Henry. My enthusiasm for the coming escape remained undiminished.

The only dampening of the spirits occurred when I was forced to visit our house to collect the rest of my belongings, which were to be packed in a trunk and sent ahead by road. It was here, amongst all that was familiar, that my taste for adventure began to wane a little. It was no loss to leave Margaret's clinical prison of a flat, but here it was different. The desire to cling to the floating wreckage of my past life was very strong indeed. And yet the house itself was like a corpse. In appearance it remained exactly the same, down to the last detail, but the spirit which had made it live was gone. My throat started to hurt so I hastily began to pack, just this once appreciating Margaret's fussing, for left to my own devices I would merely have sat in the middle of the floor, quite lost.

All my clothes were packed, together with many of my books and toys, and anything else that I might need. Everything else was to go into storage when the house was sold. It would all be sorted out one day, but by the time my trunk was full and my room nearly empty, apart from the bare bones of the furniture, I was more than glad to get out of the house and head back across town.

My last few days in Edinburgh passed quite pleasantly. Margaret indulged me like the condemned man that she obviously thought I was, perhaps in the hope that this treatment would compare so favourably with what was to come that I would feel compelled to run away and come back to her. We shopped for anything that I might need, as well as a few things that I wouldn't, and she even submitted to the ultimate sacrifice of cooking my favourite, and for her painfully simple, meals.

One such meal was served up on my last night at the flat. We ate together round the dining-table and, at the end of the meal I was presented with a small parcel, 'So you will remember us.' It was a wrist watch, a handsome-faced piece with a plain black strap. Impending absence makes the heart more tolerant and I was almost moved. I thanked them profusely and even went as far as saying how sad I was to go etc. In the heightened emotional atmosphere of the moment even this blatant lie was allowed to pass.

I slept lightly that night, feeling excited and perhaps just a little

33

nervous. I woke early the next morning. It was another glorious day, the rooftops were framed in blue and there was a definite spring in my step as I entered the kitchen for breakfast. Peter was taking the morning off work to see me onto the train. I was to catch a train at just after one, as Uncle Henry was to make a rare appearance in the civilised world and accompany me on the journey back. Margaret didn't seem too pleased about this but I had never travelled much, and would be grateful for some company.

We spent the morning making last minute preparations and chatting in the flat. Margaret assured me that if there was anything I needed or (hopefully) if I wasn't happy, then I mustn't hesitate in getting in touch. She then began trying to worry me by changing her tack of the last week and giving firm assurances that Henry wasn't all that bad and that she was sure that a brave lad like me would soon get used to him. Perhaps. But even this new approach failed to daunt me and I glanced impatiently at my new watch as the morning slowly passed.

We drove to the station in silence. The town was crowded and we made slow progress through the traffic. From the back seat it was almost possible to see Margaret's hackles rise as the station came into view. Having pounced on a parking space my baggage was lifted out of the boot and we made our way towards the appropriate platform.

Stations have a marvellous air of neutrality about them, a sense of being detached from the town in which they just happen to stand, and great vistas open out under their dirty roofs as place names flicker past on the departure boards. Once a train is boarded it is almost an anti-climax to be able to travel to just one of these destinations. As I looked around me I began to feel quite elated. I may have had no past to cling to, but here lay a whole world to be explored. I knew little of the world that I was about to enter.

We arrived at the barrier with ten minutes to spare. Margaret was obviously not keen on the idea of waiting around, which suited me fine. There is nothing worse than sitting in a train, going through an exaggerated routine of making oneself comfortable, then exchanging inane grins with the person who stands outside in a fidget of embarrassment waiting for the wretched thing to go. Margaret surveyed the platform with great caution, squinting at the many figures that loaded themselves into the carriages. Then she almost jumped and whispered conspiratorially to Peter 'There he is.'

I followed her gaze and found a solitary figure, familiar only from descriptions, standing out from the rest of the clattering crowd. He was a tall man, very distinguished-looking, his hair and beard a uniform shade of silver, his long frame carefully dressed in a suit of well-cut tweed. He was examining a watch, which he closed and replaced in his waistcoat pocket before looking up.

'He's seen us,' Margaret whispered, and, before I had a chance to say a word, I had been kissed on the cheek with alarming rapidity then propelled down the platform with a push and a quiet farewell. Now, I was never one for protracted goodbyes, but this seemed ridiculously brief even by my standards. I made my solitary way down the platform like some political prisoner being exchanged across a bleak German bridge. I stopped and looked back, only just catching sight of Peter waving as Margaret hauled him like a troublesome toddler into the shelter of the crowd. Of Margaret I could see only a resolute back.

Somewhat bemused, I turned to pick up my case, and, bending down, I found myself staring into a pair of sturdy brown shoes, whose high polish reflected the beams and arches of the station roof. A pigeon flitted from toe to toe, vanishing briefly between feet. Above me I found a pair of grey eyes regarding me with a calm, and rather cold expression, set on either side of a well-bred nose. An educated voice spoke from within the large, but tidy, beard.

'There you are, boy. Come along now, we haven't got all day.'

He picked up my case in a long, clean hand and I followed him without a word down the platform. As he stepped up onto the train he turned as I waited to follow him. He looked me up and down with a slight nod of the head.

'Yes. How typical of your father to die while it was still unfashionable.'

And hello Uncle Henry.

eight

In which I long for the frying-pan

During the course of the train journey any doubts that I may have had about Uncle Henry soon disappeared. They were replaced by what might best be described as terror. It wasn't that Uncle Henry said anything unpleasant or at all alarming, in fact it was quite the opposite. For over an hour after the journey began he did not say a single word, but sat opposite me engrossed in a book, occasionally making marks in the margin with a small black pencil which he would produce from the breast pocket of his jacket then replace carefully without looking up. Very rarely would his head lift to check our position through the window, once or twice glancing in my direction to be met by an instinctive distortion of the face which I intended to be a smile.

I was just not used to this sort of behaviour. It is the child's lot to be at all times engaged in some form of verbal exchange. He is questioned, coaxed, teased, chided, sometimes even allowed to take part in a real conversation. This pattern of constant forced communication was one that I had always found tiresome and often extremely awkward, but this was something else again. This was not a sulk, nor an embarrassed pause when conversation runs out. This was genuine one hundred per cent pure silence. And silence is cumulative in its effect – the longer the silence, the harder it is to break, so my voice crept further and further back from my mouth until a clearing of the throat became a deafening ordeal.

I thought that maybe if I were to read too then the tension might be relieved a little, but my book was in one of my bags on the luggage rack, so I would have to stand up to get it. In the atmosphere of that railway carriage even a movement as simple as that seemed quite daunting, so I stayed where I was. The arrival of the guard provided a bit of variety. Instead of plain fear I was now able to experience panic, as I had no ticket. I feared the worst, but Uncle Henry wordlessly handed over two tickets and the guard had no need to drag me away to some dreadful punishment. Instead, comforted by the second ticket, which proved that my existence was being acknowledged to at least that extent, I grew bold enough to stand up and haul my bag off the luggage rack, nearly braining the elderly lady on my right in the process. I managed to dig out my book and began to read.

By this time we were crossing into Fife by means of that overgrown Meccano set and painter's nightmare, the Forth bridge. Far below, blinking through the girders like a peepshow, a long black shape, far darker than the shadow of the bridge, moved ominously towards the open sea from the naval dockyard upstream. As it passed beneath us a chill crept up through my stomach, but that was nothing in comparison to the acres of gooseflesh generated when I looked up. I saw that Henry's eyes were trained on the same place below, but there was no chill in his guts, not if the small smile that crept across his face was anything to go by. He returned to his book, settling back in his seat with the satisfied air of a man for whom everything is going to plan.

I tried to continue with my reading, but found myself compulsively looking up, hoping to see that smug expression fade from his face, but Uncle Henry merely surveyed me with clinical disinterest and made another mark in the margin.

Had the journey continued in this vein much longer I think I might well have cracked and run gibbering from the carriage. It had the nightmare atmosphere of a Hitchcock thriller. There I was, trapped with the most evil man in the world while none of the vacantly dozing grannies around me even realised. Who would believe me if I did say anything? As if I would dare anyway. Aunt Margaret, why have you forsaken me? I was steadily working myself into a state when the routine was broken. The train ahead of us had broken down and its passengers were to be transferred into our already crowded carriages. The platform at Perth was a sea of disgruntled faces, who were in self-righteous mood as they boarded with much watch-tapping and tales of worried relatives at the other end. It was soon standing room only in our carriage. The aisle was awash with elderly ladies and their luggage. They were obviously travelling together for they were organised by a pack leader, the dominant member found in any group, who placed them in seats vacated by the more gallant gentlemen. I was able to number myself amongst them, for I rose quickly, relieved to escape from Henry's oppressive silence. Within a few minutes there were but two ladies still standing – and one gentleman still seated. He ignored them totally, seemed not to have noticed my transformation into a green twin-set, and made another mark in the margin.

And then the trouble began. The pack leader was standing near Uncle Henry with her back to me as I stood by the door. I could not see her face, only the fox stole which hung across her shoulder, so that when she began to speak she gave the impression of a second-rate ventriloquist. Her's was a loud and painful voice with the laboured refinement of a Morningside / Kelvinside / pain in the backside accent, a high suburban whine like a wasp trapped in a sherry bottle. She addressed her one still upright companion.

'Are you sure that you're all right standing up like that? With your leg and all. Let me know if you feel at all strained. I'm sure that some kind person will give you a seat.'

Uncle Henry made another note. She was not going to be ignored.

'It's a long journey to Inverness, isn't it?' There was a feeble nod from her number two, indicating no taste for trouble. 'Especially after being left standing on that hot platform for an hour. But I suppose we should be used to it by now. The age of chivalry must be dead after all.' Ho ho, a small joke. 'But one can but hope.'

At this Henry finally looked up, surveying her with an expression of mild interest in a not uncommon anthropological specimen. He began to move slightly in his chair – fox stole prepared to pounce, but Henry's shuffling resulted in nothing more than a crossing of the legs, and the turn of another page. Fox stole felt cheated, and decided to turn nasty.

'Of course, people nowadays just have no manners. Even those old enough to know better. I mean, the way we were shunted about at Perth station like animals' – the stole twitched as its name was taken in vain – 'and now left standing here in this stuffy carriage. And you with your leg. I really don't know. What is the world coming to?'

To which Henry, looking up with a smile of devastating serenity replied 'An end, Madam.' Then turned another page.

The stunned silence was broken only by a general sharp intake of breath. Even the fox gaped. Uncle Henry had spoken the unspeakable. A crowd from anywhere with a bit of spirit would have stoned the blasphemer to death, but this was British Rail, and only Henry remained outside the meniscus of horror that clung to the whole carriage.

I was as astonished as any one else. It was one thing to smile at submarines, but this was incredible. Nobody mentioned the war. I was shocked, although, at the back of my mind there niggled a certain grudging admiration for the way he had dealt with fox stole. That was one way to defuse a situation – introduce another bomb. Uncle Henry did have on his side the advantages of age and outward respectability, which allowed him to shock. The young are not able to do so, as it is expected of them, and the fulfilling of such expectation is merely tiresome. But Henry had stunned this carriage with such aplomb that, had the bomb itself dropped, I'm sure the effect would have been pitiful in comparison.

The silence continued for some time, eventually succumbing to the light rustle of polite conversation which was conjured up as a talisman against the well-dressed evil spirit who still sat, completely unperturbed, marking his margins. At the next stop several seats were vacated and I was able to return to my position opposite Henry. He noted my return and we both went back to our books. Across the aisle, fox stole and company were now all seated, and sat in silent outrage. I had the distinct impression that Uncle Henry's casual mention of the end of the world had troubled them less than his defiance in the face of their claims to the throne.

Outside, the countryside was beginning to rise and swell into mountains and, for the first time since the journey began, Henry actually spoke to me.

'We should be there in about ten minutes. Be ready.' Then more margin-marking. I was slightly taken aback that he should actually address me and also realised that by doing so he had associated me with his evil presence. On the other side of the aisle heads turned away in time with my sideways glance. Fortunately I was not to spend long as the hated accomplice, for, after a few minutes Henry carefully closed his book and placed it in his pocket. He stretched slightly and slowly uncrossed his legs. Fox stole could sense his forthcoming departure and indulged in a few parting shots. She sat back dramatically. 'Ah. A seat at last.' She had only been in it for an hour or so. She then seemed determined to prove that she had no sense of humour. Uncle Henry indicated to me that the train was slowing down for our stop. Fox stole smirked in a stomach turning way and said 'You know, I wouldn't be surprised if some people took their seats with them when they got off, just to make quite sure that no one else could have them.' Her cronies giggled. Henry had sinned. Henry had blasphemed. He was thus fair game in their eyes as they attempted to milk a little revenge from the situation. But these were rank amateurs in such matters, and they had made the mistake of tangling with a seasoned veteran. The train slowed. Uncle Henry signalled that I should stand up, so I did.

'Give me your hand, boy,' he said suddenly. A little surprised I none the less held out my hand. He gripped it tightly then began to shuffle towards the edge of the seat. Then, almost unbalancing me in the process, he laboriously hauled himself to his feet. Across the aisle the laughter had stopped.

'After you, boy.' I picked up my bags and headed for the door. Henry half-hopped into action, placing his hands on the seat backs and using them to swing himself along the aisle with pained exertion. Silence had returned until the train squealed and jolted to a halt. I struggled with the door for a while, then stepped down.

Once again – 'Give me your hand, boy.' With my help Henry lowered himself onto the platform gingerly, as if into a scalding bath. He landed a little awkwardly and winced before regaining his balance and an expression of great patience in the face of suffering. And then began the walk – and what a walk it was. Along the platform he struggled, dragging one useless dead-weight of a leg behind him. That's funny, I don't remember this happening in Edinburgh. He drew level with fox stole's window. She and her companions sat transfixed, a thousand apologies, their only possible redemption, trapped with them behind the dirty glass – their mouthings and forehead slappings unseen by Uncle Henry, who battled on bravely. It seemed that the gods were on his side, for the train began to creep forward at the same Richard III pace, keeping his victims imprisoned beside him. He pretended not to see them, but he obviously knew what was going on.

'Observe the faces, boy, desperately trying to atone for their error, eager to unload the burden of guilt which will now accompany them on the rest of their journey. They have made a mistake and are now paying for it. Their mistake was to judge someone by a single characteristic, in this case my behaviour. Sadly they now realise that they were wrong.' Still the train kept up the same painfully slow pace as Henry. 'Therein lies the great advantage of misanthropy. The misanthrope does not pick out one particular facet and thus expose himself to the risk of being mistaken. Instead he condemns humanity itself, thus becoming infallible in his judgements and, at the same time, the only true egalitarian.'

To the eternal relief of its occupants the train was at last beginning to accelerate. As it did, Henry turned to the window and smiled very sweetly. I found this as confusing as the rest of his actions and words.

'There is nothing,' he said, 'quite as effective in compounding guilt as forgiveness.'

The train pulled away from us and vanished round the bend. Henry stopped and produced his watch.

'Is that the time? Come along, boy, or we'll miss our bus.' Grabbing my suitcase he strode off towards the exit leaving me, and a porter who had approached to offer help, looking more than a little bemused. In fact, so miraculous was Henry's recovery that I had to run to catch up with him.

Our hurrying was in vain, for the bus turned up ten minutes later, a noisy red vehicle which was not of the most modern design. It bumped up to the stop in an aura of diesel fumes in the afternoon heat. Henry told me to get on board while he walked round to the back to stow my suitcase in the boot. The doors opened stiffly and I climbed up the steps into the stuffy interior. One or two hikers sat near the front, but the majority of passengers seemed to be local, judging by their chatter. I sat by the window and looked out at the hills which towered above. At least this was an improvement on the endless rooftops of home. The prospect of all this countryside to explore was beginning to cheer me up when, all of a sudden, all the voices in the bus fell silent. I looked round. Yes, it was Henry, and he hadn't even said anything other than asking for one and a half. But then, he didn't need to say anything. Henry was going home, and home is where everybody knows who you are.

nine

In which I first encounter Halfway House

The silent bus journey took about an hour, following the main road south before turning up a narrow byway which allowed only enough room for a single vehicle. This meant that any unfortunate tourist approaching from the other direction would suddenly find themselves faced by the lumbering red mass of the bus coming round a bend, with the driver in no mood for compromise. The choice for the unfortunate visitor was to reverse, as quickly as possible or drive into the ditch. As the so called 'passing places' were mere films of tarmac over the aforesaid ditch, it was usually easier for them to drive straight in and save the trouble of backing up.

On this particular journey we came across no other vehicles. It was not prime tourist country – most people headed in the other direction towards the Cairngorms. Besides, the road into the glen was a dead end, the village itself was famous for nothing (except perhaps Henry) and few people bothered with holidays during that final fraught summer. The road climbed steeply at first between the high banks of dry grass and bracken that pressed in on either side. An occasional sheep would tumble off the hillside to bounce gormlessly across the road to the sound of the driver's automatic curses and usually futile horn blasts. Up and up we climbed, reaching one false summit after another, only to see the ribbon of road rise further. The driver ground through gear changes with tooth-tingling crashes until eventually the endless grumbling of the engine had hauled us to a point where the road climbed no more. It descended about half as much as it had climbed, for the glen was set high in the hills, and from this summit the village could first be seen. It did not so much nestle amongst the hills as slouch, half-propping itself up on one side of the valley. Beyond the grey and white houses, and the plain-looking church, lay a small loch, fed by one division of the wide burn that made its intricate way down from the high point where the valley sides converged.

Perspectives changed as we wound down into the glen, the whole view at times being obscured by heather-clad spurs as we zig-zagged towards the village below. The bus eventually halted in a small yard outside an outsized old shed, above whose peeling green doors was the name of the bus company.

Uncle Henry was the first to rise from his seat. In fact he was the only one to rise from his seat, as everyone else remained exactly where they were. His footsteps echoed in the hush after the engine had expired, as he walked up to the front and down the steps onto the cracked tarmac of the yard. He was obviously going to fetch my case, for he disappeared round the back of the bus. It was then that every occupant of the bus, including the driver, rose as one and were out and off down the street at a rate of knots, only slowing down to gossiping pace when a safe distance had been covered. Taken aback somewhat, I waited for this stampede to pass before gathering my belongings together and alighting. Henry seemed not to have noticed this peculiar behaviour, or else he was quite accustomed to it, for he stood quite calmly, consulting his watch before tucking it back into his fob pocket. Picking up the suitcase he began to walk.

'It isn't too far, just far enough away from this,' he said, gesturing vaguely at the buildings around him. We carried on down the street in the opposite direction from the rest of the bus passengers who had by now disappeared up the wide High Street which curved away behind us, with one or two narrow tributaries that climbed the hill side. At the bottom of the High Street we turned right, past a large grey house which was followed by the black roof and white walls of the kirk. It was surrounded by a picket fence of medium height, and by the lych-gate stood a parish notice board. We continued past the small, neat churchyard, then along by the junction with the main road, before carrying on at Henry's uncomfortably swift, striding pace towards the other side of the narrow glen. On the edge of the village dry stone walls contained a few fields of cattle, beet and potatoes, but these soon gave way to bracken, heather and the woods which hid the loch.

Once the road had crossed the burn by means of a hump-backed bridge of weathered stone, it turned to the right and began to climb. We soon seemed to be quite high above the valley floor and could see across the village and the woods which had been obscuring the loch. After negotiating one particularly steep section, with the handles of my bag by now gnawing at my fingers, the house came into view. It was set on its own plateau, some way up the side of the glen, looking out over the rooftops and the blue of the loch. This flat piece of land extended some way behind the house, with a generous helping of trees, before the rocky face of the hillside continued its ascent.

At the front of the house was a hedge of holly, two or three feet high, with two much grander bushes standing as sentinels at the gateless entrance. We didn't use the front door but instead walked round on the gravel path to a lobby, which was built onto the left-hand side of the house. The inside of the lobby echoed the white walls of the rest of the house. It had a floor of red tiles and a row of pegs on which hung coats and hats, brollies and binoculars, and other trappings of a country gentleman. At the entrance to the house proper I stopped and wiped my feet with a scrupulousness only employed in other people's houses, then followed Henry into the kitchen. We crossed the polished wooden floor (I think it must be their relative proximity that makes children notice floors) and passed through into a large hallway, facing the inside of the front door.

'I shall show you to your room, which is in the attic,' said Henry, while I imagined being imprisoned amongst rat-ridden beams. 'It is safely away from my study' – he indicated a door that we were passing – 'and on the other side of the house from my own sleeping quarters. Despite this, I shall still expect as little noise as possible. I am accustomed to silence.'

At this moment I could barely imagine ever speaking again, let alone creating any kind of disturbance. We turned up the stairs, past a landing window which allowed a glimpse of a large garden, and on up another dark flight which I was relieved to find did not lead to the lofty dead end of the stairs in *Kidnapped*. Henry opened a white panelled door at the top of this second flight and ushered me in. He had to stoop to enter, as the door, and the ceiling, were quite low. It could almost have been designed with a child in mind. Henry pointed around him with the air of a jaded tour guide.

'This will be your room. It has a bed, a desk, bookshelves and ample cupboard space. You should find it comfortable enough. The bathroom is downstairs on the first floor and there is a sink of your own in that corner. I think that's all. I will inform you when supper is ready.' He turned to go, but stopped at the door, turning with a slightly quizzical expression.

'It is something of a mystery to me why your father should have chosen to inflict each of us on the other. But then, he always did have some funny ideas and we shall just have to put up with his absurd decision. Fortunately, the rapid and inevitable approach of Armageddon should make our time together mercifully short. I trust that you are not averse to omelettes?'

I shook my head vigorously and, with a nod, he was gone.

To my eternal relief he did not, as my imagination had been recklessly suggesting, lock the door behind him. Nor did the sloping walls begin to close in on me. But my first wild instinct was to escape, although, always having spurned the idea of joining the cub-scouts, I lacked the requisite sheet knotting techniques, so was forced to abandon this idea. Instead I decided to examine my surroundings and make the best of a bad lot. The room was pleasant enough, spacious and well lit by the dormer windows which were set on both sides of the house, allowing views of both the valley and the garden behind. There seemed to be all the furniture I could need, a bed in one corner, a desk by the front window, at the far end of the room a big dark wardrobe whose coathangers chimed gently as I opened it, and a chest of drawers, lined with clean brown paper. Oh well, if I've got to be here I might as well make myself at home.

My trunk was standing by one wall, next to one of the bookcases which contained a mixture of children's classics, works by Scottish writers, a number of reference books, including a suitably black dictionary, an encyclopaedia and several volumes on birds and animals. With these and my own, presently trunk-bound, library I would at least not be lacking in reading material. (I was quite a bookish child, which is something which I have only now learned to fully appreciate, as it allows one the luxury of enjoying a thoroughly uncivilised later youth whilst still, due to these earlier accumulations, appearing to be a reasonably well educated adult.) The unpacking of the trunk was a daunting prospect, so I decided instead to postpone it and tackle the smaller load of the suitcase, from which I began to unpack essentials.

Pyjamas were folded under the white linen of the pillow. Shoes were tucked under the bed and I even went as far as to hang some of my clothes in the wardrobe, for Uncle Henry seemed a tidy sort and I was anxious not to offend. Socks and underpants were carefully placed in the chest of drawers, along with shirts and vests. Books were stacked along the vacant shelves (I hoped I wasn't being too presumptuous by unpacking so soon) and sundry bits and pieces, which didn't belong anywhere else, found a place in the big bottom drawer. This left, at the bottom of the case, the bear. I felt that I might be in need of his company, especially the way my stomach was tingling nervously, and yet I somehow deduced that Uncle Henry was most probably not a bear-loving man, so it might be best if he kept his head down for a while. But where? Perhaps in a drawer, or under the bed, or. . . It was too late. The door opened suddenly. Henry looked down at me quizzically as I sat trying to look surprised at the discovery of a bear in my case.

'How old are you, boy?'

I excavated my first word of the day – 'Ten' – but it came out too loud and too high.

'Hmm. I know little of the development of the child, but I would have thought that you would be past the stage of stuffed toys. Especially of that hideously anthropomorphic design.'

I didn't know who was being insulted more, me or the bear, but by the time I looked up again through misting eyes, Henry was already on his way downstairs.

'Don't be long,' he called back. 'Supper is waiting.'

I sat the bear on the bed, seeing little point in hiding him now, and followed Henry down the stairs, halting briefly on the landing to sniff, on the pretence of looking out the window.

The meal passed in painful silence as Henry ate slowly and deliberately, as if unaware of my presence. I paced my own eating carefully, nervous of finishing too soon, and sipped water whenever I felt that I might be ahead. My timing proved to be immaculate and two sets of cutlery met in the middle of their respective plates with a pleasing synchronisation. The silence, however, continued. Henry sat in a state of what seemed rather like meditation, but could just as well have been digestion. I shuffled nervously in my seat and looked around. Then put my napkin, neatly folded, back on the table. Nothing broke the stillness of the room except the embarrassing gulp with which I drained my glass of water. Despite my acute discomfort, a lifetime's conditioning finally overcame my nerves with the need for politeness in the face of hospitality, no matter how grudging it may be. I risked another utterance.

'That was very nice, thank you.'

Although failing to elicit any reply, my Pavlovian platitude was enough to stir Henry into standing up and clearing the table. He carried the plates over to the sink. He was no longer wearing his jacket, but the waistcoat remained, and from its pocket the watch appeared again.

'I wish to read a little before I retire. I may listen to the news on the wireless. I trust you will be able to amuse yourself until you go to bed. I don't know what time you do so, but please bear in mind that breakfast is at eight. Sharp. Goodnight.'

He walked smartly into the hall and the study door closed behind him, leaving me still rooted at the table. My life was beginning to take on the air of some absurd fable. The boy who moaned too much about his fussing aunt and found himself catapulted to the other extreme, where his very existence was only acknowledged as a minor, and easily ignored, inconvenience. For a moment, while I sat there, I began to imagine that the whole thing was some kind of elaborate hoax or practical joke, designed to take my mind off Father's death. Perhaps any minute now Henry would come striding out wearing a red nose to share the joke with me and laugh at how easily I had fallen for it all. Then again, maybe he wouldn't.

It was beginning to grow dark in the kitchen. I was feeling a little vulnerable, so I decided to retreat to the attic room, where at least my own belongings might provide some comfort and lend more of an air of reality to the whole strange business. I climbed the stairs slowly, coughing quietly to remind myself, and perhaps Henry, that I was there. Surely he would appear again to go through the motions of 'If there's anything you need' or 'Sleep well' – anything would do. But the slight creak of the stairs was all that I could hear and the house was beginning to feel rather scary, so I wasted no more time in shutting myself into the room.

The room was grey and calm in the twilight – the kind of half-light that ignores colour in favour of depth and solidity. Outside the blackbirds were organising the day's end in their coded clicks. Quietly, I turned to my trunk, with the intention of making a start on the unpacking before I went to bed. The locks sprang open and the lid lifted with the pressure of tightly packed woollens. All these jumpers, in the middle of summer! And wellingtons. How absurd. Dafter still, I pulled out my duffle-coat, with its pockets stuffed full of gloves. As a lunatic counterpoint to the warm summer air that drifted through the window, I decided to see how many pairs of gloves I could wear at one time. And then tried to write my name, with predictably chaotic results. The addition of several jumpers and the duffle coat swelled not only my shape but also the growing sense of mild hysteria which was helping to lift the gloom of the situation a little. I would write to Aunt Margaret and tell her that I was dressing sensibly to avoid chills. But no! How could I be when, sin of sins, I wasn't wearing my vest. I fished it out of the drawer and it stretched unwillingly over the duffle coat. I sniggered and sweated in front of the mirror, pulling faces beneath the shadow of the hood, wondering if all this padding would make a jump to freedom out of the window possible.

Unfortunately, the heat soon began to detract from the joke so I removed the numerous garments with some difficulty, realising only too late that it would have been easier if I'd taken the gloves off first. How ridiculous that heap of wintery wrappings appeared. But only ridiculous in the rare heat of summer, not in the autumn or winter. The sartorial seasons were all represented in that trunk, along with all my other belongings. All that remained of my world was here. There was nothing to go back to. I was here to stay. The truth was repeating its old trick of waiting until you were laughing before coming out to trip you up. It only hurts when I laugh. And suddenly it really did hurt. I sat down on the bed, a little dazed by the realisation. This was no summer holiday, no soon to be over dental appointment. I was here to stay, and with *that man*. As I looked around at the many reminders of home that now littered the floor, I was suddenly aware that I was never going back.

The future seemed hopeless, the present unbearably bleak; even my past seemed to have healed up behind me, leaving me hopelessly stranded on the cold outside. What's more, my one last source of any satisfaction, my grudge-fuelled wait for the end of the world, was now lost to me as well. Anything that was spoken of so enthusiastically by the awful Henry could no longer be embraced without resentment. Feeling blank, and suddenly very, very tired, I undressed automatically, cleaned my teeth and crawled under the white sheets into the sole remaining solace of sleep.

ten

In which I have a rude awakening

This must be the end. The mountainside is falling, crumbling onto the house in great islands of turf and stone. And I am falling, falling, deafened by the roaring and hissing of the flames and the rumbling, crashing, rumbling of the boulders as they . . . Oh my God! What is that noise? A scramble to the window to find the mountain perfectly intact and wondering what all the fuss is about. At the other window – no great clouds rising above the hills beyond the glen. But that noise, what is that noise? As my pulse began to slow to a mere drum roll I sat myself down on the edge of the bed, head swimming from standing up too fast. It was now obvious that the sound was coming from somewhere in the house. In fact, it seemed to be emanating from behind the wardrobe.

I had never heard the like of it – a rumbling, glurping symphony of unearthly amplified flatulence. A Jonah's ear view of cetacean digestion, punctuated by sudden clangings and bumps of a metallic nature. I approached the wardrobe cautiously. A particularly explosive mechanical belch greeted me as I neared the wall. I had not noticed the trap door set high in the wall before. I reached up and opened it with a click and a creak, unleashing an even louder version of the noise and a faintly musty smell. The black space behind the door was just too high up for me to be able to see, so I

51

commandeered a chair from the desk and, standing on it, peered in. It was too dark to see anything, but there was plenty to hear. I remembered that, for some reason whose logic now evaded me, I had packed a torch, which was now in the bottom part of the chest of drawers. I rummaged around, but, by the time I had found it, the noise had all but subsided to a few irregular bumps and blurps. Climbing back up I shone the torch into the black hole. It was the remainder of the attic. There was no floor to cover the joists and the insides of the roof tiles were visible. I searched for whatever fiendish device Uncle Henry concealed in there, no doubt the cause of the villagers' suspicion (marvellous stimulators of the imagination are black, musty holes), but could find nothing. The only thing that broke the regular pattern of beams was a large rectangular box, which filled most of the corner to my left, behind the wardrobe. Disappointed, I climbed down, closed the trap door and replaced the chair. I was just reaching for my watch when the noise began again, this time in earnest. At first there was a distant rumbling which grew steadily louder. Then a shuddering, some light clangings and a repeat of the primeval glurpings, only far louder than before.

In the midst of this sonic assault I had quite forgotten about the time and Henry's breakfast ultimatum. I need not have worried. It was still only ten past six, so I had nearly two hours in which to prepare myself for the next round of mental torture. I took my dressing-gown down from the back of the door and pulled it on. Then, like some hunted creature emerging from a burrow, I opened the door and listened for any signs of life. I could hear little above the noise from the attic, so cautiously made my way down the stairs. The toilet was separate from the bathroom which was fortunate, as I was desperate and the bathroom appeared to be occupied. I could hear splashing sounds, someone quietly humming to themselves and occasional clanks and gurgles rather like those behind the wardrobe. Perched in that most thought-provoking of positions in the smallest room in the house I began to put two and two together to make 'bath'. The obscene sounds in the attic were obviously connected in some way with the plumbing. This at least solved one of my worries if not the problem of the noise itself. Next door there seemed to be signs of further activity.

There was more of an up, out and getting dried sort of a humming and I assumed that Henry must be finished with his bath. Anxious to avoid running into him I opened the door quietly, then flushed and ran. The bedroom door closed behind me just as the bathroom bolt clicked back and feet padded across the landing.

I completed my ablutions at the sink in my room, not wishing to venture downstairs and risk the possibility of meeting Henry before the certain terrors of breakfast. I still had over an hour to spare so I began to finish the unpacking that I had started the night before. Like many things which are carefully put off because of their daunting nature, the trunk took nowhere near as long to unpack as I had imagined. I made the bed carefully, checked that the room was tidy, then sat myself at the desk to have a look at the new world that I had entered. It lay before me beneath a blanket of light mist which covered the floor of the glen, hiding the village and most of the loch. I watched, half hypnotised, as the sun, creeping lazily up over the hills, began to melt the grey mass below, sending it sliding off the silver of the loch and the trees, then steadily unveiling the rooftops of the houses. It would be another fine day, weatherwise that was. Other than that I had no idea what lay in store.

I turned from gazing across the glen to the nearest of the bookshelves. A big brown volume caught my eye – *The Birds of Great Britain and Ireland, Illustrated*. I had a mild interest in ornithology which could turn to positive enthusiasm if the bird in question was large and vicious enough, the more talons the better. Here in the Highlands there would surely be all manner of birds of prey, swooping down on innocent lambs, and perhaps the occasional small child, to carry them off to its mountain lair. Or eyrie, I was sure that eagles didn't live in lairs, that was something else. Anyway, whatever they lived in I was sure there would be some around here. Perhaps even some ospreys, which would swoop down out of the sun to snatch up from the lochs and rivers unsuspecting fish, and perhaps the occasional small child. If it was swimming. This book would be able to give the relevant details of where this small air force of child-eating birds might lurk. I opened it to be met by the distinctive smell of old paper, and turned to 'O' for osprey. It wasn't there. Nor was 'E' for eagle. The birds in this book were listed under their unpronounceable, and really rather silly, Latin names. A fat lot of use. I turned instead to the index, which gave the page numbers but still only stupid Latin names. As a last resort I hoped that a contents page might be more cooperative, so turned right back to the beginning. It was in doing so that I first saw the writing on the flyleaf. Several double-takes had come and gone before I would finally accept what I had seen. There, in the corner, written in a young and simple hand, with now rather faded black ink, was my father's name along with a date that indicated that it had been written when he was about twelve. At first I was sure that I was merely managing to confuse myself. This must be one of the books from home, you just don't remember it. But no, there were all my books on that other shelf. This discovery was something of a bombshell. A whole new light was cast on everything. Up until that moment I had quite happily convinced myself that father had known as little about Uncle Henry as I did, that I was sent here because there was nowhere else to go. After all, he was my only living relative. Admittedly, Margaret had spoken ill of Henry, but to me that was as good a recommendation as anything. She hadn't even liked Father. But this was quite different. Just for once she had known what she was talking about. Uncle Henry *was* an evil old bastard, and Father was now quite plainly part of the conspiracy. Here in black and white was the evidence that condemned him. This proved that he had actually *been* here, so he must have known what Henry was like. But still he sent me here. Everything became quite clear now. It all tied in. He was always out at work because he really hated me and didn't want to come home. And I bet he cooked proper food for himself when I had gone to bed. And now this. He had probably died just to spite me. I was steadily working myself up into a full-blown self-righteous sulk when the present intervened. The time, what time is it? Watch hands hovered like the sword of Damocles, just before the fateful mark of eight o'clock. All indignation was rapidly deflated by the remarkably humbling effects of panic as I scrambled out of the door and gathered alarming momentum down the stairs. I arrived in the kitchen at a rate of knots, almost skidding to a halt on the wooden floor, panting a prayer that I wasn't too late.

Henry slowly turned from whatever he was doing to stare at me. His tone of voice was a reprimand in itself.

'Please do not stampede, boy, it alarms the cat.'

The cat? Indeed, there it was, a momentarily startled black creature who decided that I was no threat and continued his love affair with Henry's left leg. Henry carried the saucer out to the lobby and placed it on the floor. He pointed down to the guzzling animal.

'This is Oscar. He is, as you may have gathered, a cat. He is affectionate only when hungry. However, lacking anything that might approximate to intelligence he cannot be accused of ulterior motives or any of the other attributes which make our own species so unbearable. His greed is always transparently clear, isn't it you cretinous feline?' This appellation was one to which Oscar seemed to respond, for he mewed sycophantically and continued to tuck in noisily. Henry closed the door on him and returned to the preparation of our breakfast.

'I'm never quite sure why I keep him. In theory he keeps the house free of mice. But this means that I have to keep feeding him, otherwise he would wander off to hunt elsewhere. Of course, once he has been fed he can't be bothered to catch any mice anyway, and is thus entirely useless. Were I not averse to such things I would probably eat him.'

Whilst on the topic of eating, Henry served up breakfast, which consisted of a large quantity of toast, along with jars of home-made jam and marmalade and a bowl of apples.

'On colder mornings I make porridge, but this will do in the present climate.' I wasn't likely to disagree. Henry sat down to eat in the silence to which I had been growing accustomed until this surprisingly loquacious introduction to the house's only other occupant. However, it turned out to be a freak incident, for breakfast concluded in the same taciturn way, Henry's only words coming as he left.

'I trust that you will be able to amuse yourself. Please avoid charging downstairs, I find it extremely irritating.' Never had such a calm and quiet 'please' sounded quite so menacing. I climbed the stairs in church mouse silence and wondered what to do with the day.

eleven

❦

In which my horizons widen

Still trembling from the terrors of breakfast I sat down at the desk and looked out across the glen once more. In the sunshine the beauty of the hills was quite breathtaking. I had to keep reminding myself that it was really out there. Just as I kept trying to forget that I was here in the house with Henry. Never before had I been surrounded by so much lovely and exciting scenery. But never before in my life had I come across someone like Henry Dundas. How I would love to live amongst such hills. But with him? A battle was raging which, given the confined space of the head in which it took place, was making me feel dizzy. The hills were all very well but, that awful silence at the table. And the frightening nature of the few words that were spoken, well . . . No. It wasn't worth it. From the drawer I removed the pad of paper that I had placed there whilst unpacking. I lay it on the desk and began to write. It was to be a letter to Aunt Margaret, who now compared almost favourably with Henry and my newly revealed traitor father.

Dear Margaret,
    You were right. He is an evil old man and he doesn't speak to me and when he does it's always to say something horrible.

I'm lonely and frightened and I hate it here and want to come back to live with you . . .

With you? In that flat in the middle of the city? With all that tortuously contrived food? And your constant fussing? What am I saying? Get a grip, boy. It isn't that bad yet. Shaking myself back to some semblance of sense I turned the paper over and began to draw on the back. I drew the shape of the hills, and became quite lost in their curves and hollows, their bold Gothic outcrops and distant streaks of burns.

I was to spend several days at that desk, watching the shadows change the shapes and forms of the landscape, copying pictures out of books, reading, or just doing nothing. At first I felt no desire to leave the confines of the house. I still felt rather shaken by everything that had happened, and was still happening. I also felt rather tired and found the quiet rest helpful in preparing myself for the next round with Henry.

No ten-year-old boy can stay indoors too long, not with a summer like that going on without him. After a while the room began to contract and seem dark and dull compared to the world outside the windows, especially the tree-dappled garden which looked so tempting and idyllic. I began to long for fresh air and, still a little too tired and timid for exploring, decided that the long lawns and sheltered corners of the garden would be as good an introduction to the outside world as any. One morning, after wakening to the regular clarion of the boiler, I decided to break the breakfast silence with a tentative question.

'Uncle Henry?'

'I would be grateful if you would refrain from using that particular title, boy. I mean, can you honestly imagine anyone less avuncular than myself?'

I wore my non-comprehension plainly across my blank face.

'What I mean, boy, is that I would be pleased if you did not call me "Uncle". If anything, my name should suffice. Besides, given that there are but two of us in the house I very much doubt if there will be much confusion over who is addressing whom.'

'Well, no. I mean yes, there won't be. Thank you.' I had quite forgotten about my initial enquiry.

'Now what were you going to say, boy?'

'Say? Well, I . . . Oh yes. I was going to ask if it would be all right, that is, if you don't mind, if I went out into the garden. Sometimes.' Henry was already on his way out when he replied.

'As long as you don't disturb me, and attend meals punctually, I don't really care what you do.' He was gone, and I breathed a sigh of relief, even allowing myself a slight smile at this small step forward in communications, no matter how coldly it may have occurred.

I fetched my scribbling pad from my room and took it, and some books and pencils, down the stairs, quietly past the study, through the kitchen and out into the garden. The warmth of the sun on my face began to lift my sense of gloom and I set about finding a likely spot to settle down. It was a large garden, sheltered by a high wall of weathered brick, unusual in these stonebuilt parts. A number of mature trees, some oaks and sycamores and, beyond the wall Scots pine, added further shelter from the wind. Not that there was much wind to ruffle the branches of the trees or blow across the long lawns or vegetable patches. By the vegetables were a clump of raspberry bushes, protected by nets, and beyond them in the corner stood a shed and, within a wire compound, a felt-roofed chicken coop, outside which a motley assortment of about half a dozen fowls strutted around in the sun.

In the opposite corner from these out-buildings lay a place which I soon claimed as my own. It was a long way from the house, hidden away behind some trees, and, as well as being quite private, caught a good deal of the sun. This corner became a haven away from the dark interior of the house. I sometimes had some company there when Oscar, relinquishing his usual perch atop the coal bunker, would join me in the shade of the trees, more often than not lured by the presence of cheese sandwiches which, if prepared at breakfast time, allowed a respite from lunch, which Henry could rarely be bothered to make.

There was one slight hitch. A garden of that size does not look after itself. Taking a break from whatever occupied him in his study, Henry would appear at various times of the day to tend the vegetables, feed the chickens or mow the lawns with a noisy old petrol mower. I didn't like to remain in the garden while he was there, so we acted like some elaborate mechanical barometer, one disappearing inside as the other emerged from the house.

I would watch Henry from the back window of my room, waiting patiently for him to return to his study. I wasn't sure what he did in there – read and made notes in books, I assumed. In braver moments I would halt briefly outside the study door to listen to the ominous drone of the wireless, but these stops were short. I was soon propelled away by the blackness of the snippets that I overheard and the fear of bumping into Henry, so I built up only a vague and reluctant picture of the terminal fever that was gripping the world outside the glen.

As for the world inside the glen, I knew very little of it other than what I had seen from the window and from the bus and walk on the day I arrived. Acclimatised by my days in the garden I began to long for a further expansion of my horizons. I waited for another of the cheese sandwich days and, having decided that Henry's 'I don't care what you do' constituted sufficient licence, I went out through the lobby and round to the front of the house. Beyond the holly bushes the road led to the right, down towards the village, or petered out to the left, becoming a narrow sheep track which edged up the hill, intersecting in places with similar paths. I began to climb, at first with the intention of conquering the mountain which provided the back drop for the house, but settling after about an hour for an outcrop of rocks a few hundred feet up.

Even higher up the air was quite still. Crickets would stop their songs until I had safely passed, then continue with their chirping. Perched on some springy turf atop the outcrop I could see right down into the garden below. There was my corner, and just visible beneath the plum trees was the coal bunker. A miniature Henry appeared from the back of the doll's house and walked across to the chickens. He vanished into the coop then reappeared after a moment preceded by a characteristically flustered chicken. It all looked so very small. I found it hard to imagine that there was room in that tiny building (the house, not the chicken coop) for the dark mass of atmosphere that hung over me and amplified my every sound and movement with nervous self-consciousness. The tiny Henry was crossing back over the lawn now, and soon disappeared into the house.

I decided to continue my ascent but was detained after several yards by an interesting bed of quartz, in which I tried to start a small mine with a piece of rock. After losing interest in vandalising the mountain I began to climb once more, up a little, then along a bit, all over the face of the hill. I rolled small stones down the slope, watching them bounce their way towards the glen until smothered by the heather. I made what I took to be authentic rabbit noises down burrows, but received no reply. On I wandered, carefully skirting round patches of undoubtedly adder-infested bracken. If I was bitten in the foot, would it be possible to suck the poison out without dislocating something?

I reached yet another false summit on the hill. It dipped slightly into a small valley before climbing again sharply to the mountain top. Above me a buzzard circled, drifting lazily on the warm air, no doubt in search of small children. At this height the house was hidden by the lower parts of the hill, as was most of the valley floor with the exception of one end of the loch. The buzzard was right above my head now. I guarded my sandwiches until it had floated away, then sat down and began to eat. The day was very warm and drowsy. Bees hummed past through the heather bells and I lay back to watch the sky drift by.

I must have dozed for some time, for the sun had moved significantly when I opened my eyes. A slightly panicky look at my watch showed me that I had an hour to climb down. I strode down with renewed confidence towards the tiny house, wondering how on earth I had found it so frightening. It soon reminded me, by growing bigger and bigger as I approached. In fact, by the time I reached the hedge I was sure that it was a good deal larger, and darker inside, than it had been when I left. It was hard to maintain my air of perspective without the aid of a passing mountain, and most of my new-found optimism had evaporated by the time supper finished in its usual icy silence.

twelve

❧

*In which there is a variation
on the rude awakening*

On the following morning something very strange happened. Nothing to be precise. Nothing was the strange thing that happened, if you see what I mean. I rolled over in bed, scratched in vain at an inaccessible mid-lumbar itch, then went back to sleep on my arm, wakening to find it dead to the world. I prodded and waggled it about a bit, yawned, opened my eyes and looked around. It was already light, so I reached over to find out what time it was. Either it was 8.45 or my watch had a very sick sense of humour. I sprang from the bed in a tangle of sheets and a cold sweat. Rushing to the door I dragged on my dressing-gown and ran halfway down the stairs, then back up, then a quarter of the way down again then up once more in a high-speed Busby Berkely routine of indecision as to whether the sin of lateness could be further compounded by arriving in pyjamas. I opted in the end for clothes and, after much frantic sock-hopping, scrambled downstairs as quietly as I could and entered the kitchen a full fifty-five minutes late, looking not unlike someone who has dressed in a minute and a half. It was when I halted there, in the middle of the floor, and could hear above my panting, that I noticed the strange sound – the distinctive noise of nothing happening. The plumbing was not indulging in its usual dawn fanfare. No wonder I had slept in. What's more, the kitchen was empty, no Henry to be seen. He was not in the garden either, where Oscar was ineffectually stalking a bird. I turned to find a note on the table, propped against the fruit bowl.

I have gone out for the morning. Necessary foodstuffs will be found in appropriate cupboards. I shall be back later this afternoon.

Henry.

Now this was a turn up for the books. A morning by myself. Well, I did spend every morning by myself, but today I would be spared any contact with Henry. I would be able to enjoy the garden without the usual ritual of using it in shifts. I would spend the morning there, then at about lunchtime I would eat and set out on another journey into the surrounding countryside, thus avoiding Henry all day until suppertime. That was a delightful prospect.

It was a pleasant, peaceful morning. Oscar and I shared some toast in the garden and played a game with a piece of grass until my hand was over-enthusiastically pounced upon, when I returned indoors to wash my plate and cup. From the shelf in my room I fished out an ordnance survey map of the area with which to plan my route, and one of Father's books on birds, even though it still had not been forgiven for being there. Back in my corner of the garden I opened out the map. After persuading Oscar that this was not another game, I planned my route for the afternoon. I noted that, as well as the path that led up the hillside, there was another track that led down from our plateau to the side of the loch. It lay behind a copse, several yards from the house. I remembered the trees from my previous expedition and had a pretty good idea where the path must start, even though I had not actually noticed it. I decided that this would be today's route and examined it carefully, becoming engrossed in the details of the map, which became a world in itself.

Several small pebbles, of clearly bad intent, were attempting to invade the valley while I, in the guise of a piece of twig, attempted to defend the village. Single-handed of course. In the end, although greatly outnumbered, I managed to cunningly out-manoeuvre them, leading them to their doom over the eternal chasm of the edge of the map. But injustice was still ripe in the rest of the universe. On the strange and distant planet beneath the tree, a small colony of daring space explorers had set up their city of dome buildings (not unlike acorn cups in their design) in the shadow of the mighty mountains of the mysterious oak-root range. All was quiet until, suddenly, over the mountains appeared the menacing giant figures of the dandelions of death, a race of evil man-eating plants from near the wall. All looked lost until, yes! It's wonder-twig. Only he can save them. Which of course he did, single-handed, but not without a fierce and merciless struggle. He was just turning to bid the citizens farewell before tackling evil in some other corner of the galaxy, when he saw, to his horror, the entire galactic village being annihilated by the black paw from beyond. Stupid cat! Why don't you get back to your coal bunker?

Oscar padded off, showing absolutely no signs of remorse for the cataclysm he had just caused. He had no interest in the thousand worlds within a garden that I could see with my child's eye. I often wonder if it's just growing taller that lifts us from the ground. If that were the case then by simply bending down we would be able to return to the world we knew as children, the land of counterpane and the world within a grain. But, alas, it seems we cannot. And doesn't it get us into some right pickles? Like the end of the world. When a whole planet lay amongst the pebbles by a tree root, how vast and unassailable that tree seemed. The felling of that tree really would have seemed like a cataclysm. And how many trees in a glen, and how many glens in the world? Perhaps it wasn't just ignorance and wilful avoidance of the truth that made me far less perturbed than the adults were about the approaching war. Perhaps to the child's mind the whole thing is quite simply beyond comprehension, and thus impossible to take seriously. The child's eye for the most minute of worlds is what gives him his sense of wonder and what makes the world at large so unbelievably vast and glorious. Starting with the silvery hairs in the feathered grain of that blade of grass right in front of my nose, how vast would be the sheet of paper required to map this corner, let alone the whole garden or the world beyond it. And just how sadly lacking in any such sense of wonder would be the hand that could crumple it all up and fling it onto the fire.

But this is all hindsight. At the time I was busy wondering just what kind of hand could take an ordnance survey map and fold it back into its cover without creating several new Highland faultlines. After trying more permutations than actually seemed possible I settled for a reasonable likeness to the original shape, give or take a bulge or two.

There was just time to make something to eat and then be gone before Henry could possibly return. I set about a thorough search of the cupboards and fridge. There were many jars containing pickled onions and beetroot from the garden. Several others contained the jam made from last year's raspberries. There were bags of flour, some dried yeast and big brown eggs, with feathers still clinging to them, dates carefully pencilled onto the shells, stacked in a row along a rack on the shelf. On the floor by the fridge stood a basket of fresh runner beans and inside the fridge there was a hefty cheese. This was all very well, but I fancied something different in my sandwiches, ham or fish paste, something like that. But my search proved fruitless, nay, meatless. It then dawned on me that not once had we eaten at any of our meals so far, any kind of meat. This was odd, especially after the roasts, steaks and bacon butties that father usually managed to burn. How peculiar – not the sort of thing I would have expected from Henry at all. This was more like Aunt Margaret's sort of line, to go with the muesli (which I had, to Margaret's great annoyance, likened to squirrel sick) and all the other healthy but inedible stuff that she had inflicted on me. I had to settle for cheese and, finding the bread knife in a drawer, mutilated the loaf into a doorstep sandwich.

Gathering up map, sandwich and bird book, in case I should see any interesting wildlife, I set off down the path to the loch. At first it passed through a group of tall trees, real Scots pines and not the hideous Scandinavian Christmas trees with which the Forestry Commission have tried to turn the Highlands into one vast, deodorant or air freshener commercial. The sun slanted in beams which picked up the dust raised by my feet from the path, then beat down fully as I stepped out from the shade. The path was steep in places and sometimes a bit crumbly due to the dry summer but, slowly and steadily, I made it down to the floor of the glen. From down here the loch seemed surprisingly large. One end was sheltered from the village by plumes of deciduous woodland, while the other narrowed into a long finger surrounded by marshy beds of reeds. The sun danced across the water as I placed my bundle of food and paper on a nearby boulder and began to search for flat stones. I gathered up a handful and then, with a deft flick of the wrist, sent one flying out across the water to bounce once, sideways, before vanishing without further ceremony. Other attempts were more successful, sending dark shapes skimming out towards the middle of the loch, until one particularly enthusiastic effort resulted in no less than seven bounces (if you counted the one when it sank) and a nasty clicking noise in my wrist, so I decided to stop before I lost the use of my right hand.

Wandering along the shore a little I came to a flat topped boulder, about a foot from the shore. One leap saw me safely on to it and I settled down on the warm rock to watch for birds, or any monsters of the Ness variety that might have migrated south to avoid publicity. The only long neck I saw in the loch belonged to a heron, standing frozen on one leg up by the reeds. In a slow, clockwork way it waded towards the shore before unfurling like a great umbrella, sweeping across the air with broad, curved wings. A slight breeze rose, as if created by the heron's mighty wings, and began to move small waves across the loch towards me. In the shallow water in front of me the faces of the approaching waves would suddenly give a crystal-clear glimpse of the round stones and pebbles on the floor of the loch, almost gold in the sunlight, before dissolving into the flickering grey and silver illusion of the surface. I watched these little flashes of reality as I sat on my boulder, attempting to wrap my mouth round the uneven landscape of my sandwich. I chewed and pondered for a while, thinking once more about the book, the one with Father's name in it. Hypnotised by the ripples and the sun I felt calmer and less aggressively defensive than I had done before. I thought more clearly about what I had first regarded as a betrayal. Perhaps I had been a little hasty. I still couldn't figure out why Father had sent me up here, unless there was just nowhere else to go. I couldn't think of anywhere else, other than Margaret's, and Father had known that I didn't like her. He didn't send me there because he knew . . . maybe he did send me here because he had no idea what Uncle Henry was really like. All right, so he had been here, but that was a long time ago. He might only have been here once. Or maybe Henry had changed over the years. I began to feel rather guilty about jumping to conclusions and, very magnanimously, decided to give Father the benefit of the doubt. This made me feel a great deal better about the whole business, if a little sad that I had had to come here at all.

The rest of the afternoon was spent in the infinitesimal potterings that characterise the child's day. I wandered some distance along the shores of the loch and felt pleasantly tired by the time I began the climb back up to the house.

If it is at all possible to detect any change of mood in someone whose face remains passive at all times and who rarely if ever speaks to you, then I am sure that Henry seemed a little subdued when I arrived in the kitchen just before supper time. He didn't even bother to kick Oscar out of the way when he bothered away at his feet. I was slightly early for supper and sat down in the kitchen to wait. Henry left the potatoes simmering and vanished briefly into the study where I could hear the sound of the radio. When he emerged he seemed a little happier and I assumed that he must have been worrying because things had been taking a turn for the better but had now returned to their usual ever darkening course. In spite of this his voice seemed a little quieter and less dramatic than usual when we exchanged our only words of the meal.

'I trust that you managed at breakfast and lunch?'

'Yes, thank you.'

'Good. It has always been my belief that the man who doesn't know how to cook for himself deserves to starve.'

Now where had I heard that before?

thirteen

*In which I have some contact with
the outside world*

Perhaps it was the lack of a bath that had dampened Henry's spirits, for he seemed to have recovered by the following morning, when the boiler once more sang out in the early hours. I could hear him humming in the bathroom from the neighbouring toilet. Bad timing on my part resulted in us both appearing on the landing at the same time, but Henry ignored me and went off, still humming quietly, to his room.

Although I had been in the house for over a week I myself had yet to use the bath. At home this would have been something of an achievement, but here, where no rules stated bed-time or bath-time, there was no fun in trying to avoid it. I decided, for the first time quite voluntarily, to have a bath. Sometime. I broached the subject at breakfast, to be told that as long as I left the bath clean and did not, under any circumstances, leave the boiler on for more than half an hour, I was welcome to bathe at any time that did not coincide with Henry's regular ablutions. This created no problems, as I had always failed to see the point of having a bath first thing in the morning, when you hadn't even had time to get dirty. I would get round to it one evening. Sometime.

In the meantime, a wash at the sink usually sufficed, and I had planned a swim in the loch one day, when it didn't look too cold. But today I was unsure. I didn't feel in a particularly exploratory mood and the sky had finally broken its run of perfect blue days. I sat myself at the desk and decided that I really ought to write to Aunt Margaret. A 'thank you for having me' letter was well overdue and would help to allay any fears about my welfare which might result, God forbid, in a visit. Spurred on by this thought I began to write. I had got as far as the address and the 'Dear Aunt Margaret' when I began to feel that something was wrong. Pencils. That was the problem. You can't go writing letters with pencils. Not when you're ten. Father had given me a fountain pen for my birthday, but with his usual lack of mental presence, had forgotten to provide any ink. This left two alternatives: either to engrave the letter on something, or find some ink. There was only one thing for it. A trip to the village was in order. There was sure to be a shop there of some description. This became quite an exciting prospect. A shop might well contain chocolate and comics, books and perhaps even stationery! I still had some money, given to me by Aunt Margaret when I left, and this seemed like as good a time as any to spend some of it. After all, I might as well enjoy myself before the end of the world arrives.

It was a grey morning when I set out down the hill to the village. Mist had crept down from the hill tops to fill the valley. I even contemplated taking my duffle coat, so dismal a day was it, but settled instead for a light waterproof. By the time I reached the floor of the glen the mist was very thick, so I wasted no time in crossing the bridge, passing the church and turning into the main street. There was the yard where the bus had stopped, and a little further up was a pub called the White Stag, with a badly painted sign depicting just such a beast. From the chimneys of the houses percolated the autumnal smell of coal fire smoke mingling with mist as I continued up the High Street. After about a hundred yards I came to what was obviously a shop window. It contained all the requisites of a rural general store; stacks of tins with sun-faded labels, out of date boxes of breakfast cereal, pink plastic rainhats and hairgrips, a few hopeful postcards of the Cairngorms and the obligatory sprinkling of dessicated wasps. The entrance was around the corner in a lane just off the main street. In the insipid turquoise frame of the door there was a plate of glass, onto which were stuck numerous advertisements for everything from home-made jam to the services of an adolescent baby-sitter (allergic to dogs.) The door opened with a rattle and the ringing of a bell, faces turning to view this small stranger before returning to village gossip.

Before me was a wide counter, covered by a selection of news-papers and magazines, to the right a tiny post office section and to the left the shelves of the general store. One wall was taken up by sundry items like string and paper, glue and pencils. I managed to track down a dusty box, inside which was a squat bottle of black ink. On impulse I also picked up an interesting notepad, with hard covers like a book (the kind of purposeless purchase which has, over the course of my life, led to one of the largest collections of virgin stationery in the Western hemisphere).

Faced by a tray of confectionery I felt suddenly profligate and selected two rather large bars of chocolate. I carefully placed my bundle on the counter. A short, round man, with a face like a bruised beetroot, smiled at me from behind the counter, breaking off from sympathising with an elderly couple about a recent plague of greenfly which had turned the garden into an absolute nightmare.

'Now then, young man, what can we do for you?' he asked in his sing-song voice.

'I'd like these please,' I replied, stating the obvious.

'Certainly.' He picked up the chocolate with a patronising 'Oh! I hope you won't be making yourself sick?' I shook my head. 'Or fat like me' – he patted his round belly to appreciative little laughs from the old couple. I smiled politely. Next came the notebook and ink. 'Ah. So it's a book you're writing is it? In hardback as well. You will have to give me some copies, to sell in the shop, when it's finished.' The elderly couple beamed indulgently as I squirmed in embarrassment. For once Henry's silence seemed like a blessing. 'Now then, is there anything else you would like?'

'No, thanks. That's all.'

'Right, well we'll just work this out.' Whilst he added up the sum on the back of a paper bag I fumbled in my pocket for some money. The elderly lady spoke.

'You can always draw some nice pictures in your book when you're stuck inside on a day like this.'

'Aye, it's miserable, isn't it?' continued the shop-keeper, filling a candy-striped bag with my purchases. 'You'll be on holiday here, will you?' as I handed over the money.

'No. Actually I've come to live here.'

'Really?' The till rang. 'Well, isn't that grand?'

'And what do you think of our wee glen?' asked the lady.

'It's very nice, thank you.'

'Aye, it's a grand place, is it not?' the shop-keeper said, picking out my change. 'And where is it that you're staying?'

'With my uncle.'

'Oh, your uncle, that's fine. And where about does he live?'

'Erm, up the hill. At Halfway House.' The silence prepared for the ceremonial dropping of the pin was broken instead by the clatter of coins on the floor.

'Oh. Silly me. I've dropped your change.' He vanished behind the counter like a captain going down with his ship. The old lady swallowed hard.

'Halfway House, did you say?' she pronounced the name like the hunch-backed Transylvanian peasant who hangs around at the mist-wreathed station being asked directions to Castle Frankenstein.

'Yes. That's right.'

'With your . . . uncle?' the shopkeeper emerged again.

'Yes . . . ' I was beginnng to feel nervous as well as embarrassed. The old man spoke for the first time as another shopper stood frozen behind me with a tin of peas.

'And how do you like living there? With your uncle?' I sensed faint menace in his voice and felt that I had better think carefully. All eyes were upon me. Give the wrong answer and they might think me in cahoots with Henry, or perhaps even possessed. I didn't relish the prospect of being stoned to death or burned at the stake if I gave the wrong answer but, in spite of this, a certain family loyalty took hold of me. Even cold blood is thicker than water.

'It's . . . fine, thank you. I like it.'

It was not what they wanted to hear. The shop-keeper's voice had changed dramatically.

'Aye. Well, don't forget your change.'

I picked up the money and my parcel. It seemed to be a long walk to the door, my footsteps the only sound until the bell tolled my passing out into the street. I began to walk very quickly through the mist.

It was not until I reached the bridge that I slowed from my forced march. There must have been rain in the night, for the burn was in spate, impatiently rushing over rocks and tugging at plants on the bank in its hurry to get under the bridge and away from this gloomy spot. I was astonished at the way in which people in the shop had turned so quickly. I had quite forgotten about the effect that Henry could have on his neighbours. Now it seemed that even his name or just his address, was enough to invoke silence and dark faces. As I watched the smoke from the village rise over the trees I felt almost tempted to go and ask them what it was all about, why they hated him so much or, for that matter, why Henry hated them so much, and the rest of their species. Henry's behaviour, to which I had been growing accustomed, now seemed rather frightening. If he could have such an effect on so many people, then perhaps the worst was yet to come. I suddenly felt in no hurry to get back to the house and, despite the bleakness of the day, set about delaying my return as best I could.

Beside the bridge, on the village side of the burn, a stony path ran off along the bank. I was not sure where it led, but assumed that it must end up somewhere near the loch. I walked slowly with my head down, aware that, somewhere above me on the hillside, lay Henry's dark fortress. And there, within its walls, in his mysterious study, he sat, all alone, waiting for the world to die. A shiver ran up my back which even the pulling on of my waterproof failed to dispel, and I trudged on, secretly beginning to quite enjoy my misty swirl of Gothic imaginings.

Unfortunately, before I could really work myself up into a full fever of horrific speculation, I began instead to work up a sweat

71

beneath my heavy Jacobean plaid, pulled tight against the evening mists as I staggered across the endless moors to escape my evil enemies. I even began to sweat under my waterproof, which now seemed strangely out of place as the path climbed up into the sunlight. It began to fall again soon, but by now the morning mist had all but gone and the loch, as predicted, lay before me.

This was not a cheese sandwich day, so I would be obliged to turn up for lunch. For a while I was torn between fear of going back and the realisation that my eventual return was probably inevitable, and unpunctuality a grave offence in Henry's book. However, in the small space between the present and the not too distant future, it is surprising just how many obstacles can slide themselves onto one's path. On this occasion the obstacle took the form of the burn which had placed itself between me and the house. A search for stepping stones proved fruitless, and it would take too long to walk all the way back to the bridge and up the road. There was no alternative. I must leap for my life. I tucked my parcel into the pocket of my waterproof, tied the arms around my waist, and then prepared myself. Several paces back then one, two, three and actually it looks a bit narrower up there. Indeed, the turf of the opposite bank did look a bit closer a few yards upstream. I decided that, in the interests of weight and aerodynamics, I should throw the waterproof over first. I knotted it around the parcel pocket, to protect the ink then, with one careful swing of the arm, saw it land comfortably on the other side. I took this as a good omen and, ambitious to the last, stepped back three paces, cleared my throat to count, then, one, two, three and a powerful spring as, arms akimbo, our hero launches himself across the bottomless chasm to land with a satisfying thud.

The landing itself was fine. My feet were firmly planted on dry land. The only problem lay in the piece of dry land itself, a small section which appeared to feel little attachment to the rest of Mother Earth. Just as I stepped forward to reclaim my bundle, I felt the earth move. The dry earth of the bank, undermined by the burn's sudden overnight rush, peeled itself off from the rest of the glen and deposited me backside first in the sandy shallows. I sat there for a moment, quite dazed, wondering if perhaps the world had ended already, until the chill of the water around my rear quarters was enough to rouse me sufficiently to stand up and haul myself out with a few forbidden curses.

I no longer felt in any mood to hurry as I squelched up the path towards the house, and arrived at the lobby feeling cold and embarrassed. I peeped inside. Thankfully there was no Henry to be seen. Removing my socks and shoes, and shaking some of the excess water off like a dog, I crept in through the kitchen, silently past the study, and up the stairs to my room.

A quick rub down with a towel and change of clothes soon lifted the worst of the chill, but there still remained the problem of the trousers. They must hang out in the garden to dry. I reversed my stair-creeping routine and stalked once more past the study. There was still nobody in the kitchen. Out I went into the garden, intending to hang my wet clothes on a low tree branch in my corner. I glanced over my shoulder to check that Henry had not appeared in the kitchen. As I turned round I saw him, watching me from over by the vegetable patch.

'Been doing some laundry, boy?'

'Erm . . . no. I fell into the burn,' I replied, hanging my head.

'That was remarkably inept of you,' he answered, returning to whatever he was doing. 'In fact, nearly as stupid as this failed thief here.'

He was over by the raspberry bushes. Oscar sat nearby, watching the proceedings with great interest. I approached cautiously, fearing that the 'failed thief' might be some unfortunate caught in a hideous man-trap, set by Henry to protect his runner beans. Hardly less dramatic was the desperate flapping of a blackbird, who had somehow found his way under the nets, only to end up in a frenzied tangle when disturbed. Henry stood by the corner where he had ensnared himself and addressed him sternly.

'Given the amount of bread, nuts and other victuals that I provide for you and your colleagues in the bleak mid-winter, don't you feel that it might not be entirely unreasonable for me to be allowed some of my own fruit at this time of year?'

The blackbird flapped some more and stared guiltily at Henry through the black yoke of his yellow eye.

'Now stop that wretched flapping while I disengage you from the nets.' He pulled a couple of wooden pegs from the ground, lifted the nets and shuffled underneath, rising to a half crouch to reach up into the corner where the bird was trapped. Oscar spotted the opening and began to move.

'Cat. Desist.'

Who? Me? I was just on my way back to the coal bunker. His mime was not entirely convincing as he ambled off.

'Now then, keep yourself still before you damage something permanently.'

With one long hand Henry carefully enfolded the bird, holding him firmly but gently in place whilst with the fingers of the other hand he delicately unravelled head and feet from the loops of netting. Henry backed out and stood up. He held the bird close to his face. It seemed to be frozen as he spoke.

'Any more of your greed and I will take you and three and twenty of your ilk and make you all into a pie for Oscar.'

With this parting caution he tossed the blackbird into the air and watched as his dipping flight carried him away over the wall and into the trees beyond.

'There he goes. Of course, he won't learn. The next gap in the net and he'll land himself in the same pickle. But at least he won't be foolish enough to become a prisoner of memory. His whole life goes with him over the wall. All this is probably forgotten already.'

I was reminded of the episode on the railway platform, when he had gloated over the flushed faces as they were drawn along beside him. Then too he had indulged his penchant for philosophical musings, mannered and abstract in nature. He did not seem to be addressing his remarks to anyone in particular. I got the feeling that even if I had not been there he would have continued in the same vein. Perhaps it was the result of living alone with a large library of classics, and maybe my presence was purely coincidental. And yet, he almost seemed to be explaining himself, giving some insight into the workings of his mind. Then again, perhaps that too was for his own benefit.

He continued to speak to, at or over me as he carefully re-pegged the nets, crouching to search for the gap where the intruder had gained entry.

'It isn't that I am in the least sentimental about animals. They are mostly brutish and stupid. However, at least they are prepared to get on with being brutish and stupid and with a lack of self-consciousness which lends them a little charm. Sadly, the same cannot be said of our own species. We too are brutish and stupid, some too much of one to be the other. Unfortunately we fail to fulfil our destiny with the same quiet grace as other animals, constantly aspiring to higher things. Balancing on the horse's shoulders to clutch at the angels' toes as it were. There, that should do the trick.' He stood up. 'No, I am not at all sentimental about animals, I merely admire the uncontrived way in which they go about their business. And I do think it must be a terrible fate to end up inside something as pathetic as a human – which is why, in case you were wondering, I don't eat them.' The end of his sentence was heralded by a loud and particularly dissonant squawk from the chicken coop. 'Mind you, I sometimes think that the killing of chickens, like misanthropy itself, is something that could be justified on aesthetic grounds alone. Singularly ugly creature is the chicken. Anyway, lunch will be ready in about twenty minutes.' With that, he strode off back to the house.

I was left rather dumbstruck by this dramatic little speech and stood wondering whether to say 'yes', 'no', or just applaud, until I was reminded of my original mission in the garden by the steady dripping into my shoe of the wet trousers.

As I hung them lopsidedly on the line I thought over what I had just heard. Uncle Henry seemed to be saying that he didn't really like animals, but not as much as he didn't like people. Or something like that. As for this balancing on horses stuff, I surmised that perhaps he had had an unpleasant experience at a circus as a child. I shrugged and made my way indoors.

If Henry was willing to declaim at length while occupied in the garden, with his back to me, in the face to face situation of the meal table he still remained agonisingly silent and lunch was no exception.

There had been little if any improvement in communications since I had first arrived at Halfway House, but I tried to play down this side of things when I finally got around to writing my letter to Aunt Margaret. The new pot of ink came into its own, as did an inordinate number of blots and squiggles which rather detracted from the visual appeal. In spite of this I felt that I had struck just the right balance between the truth and anything that might lead her to say 'I told you so.' I ended with the assurance that if I did have any problems then she would be the first to know. But flattery gets you nowhere without a stamp. Why didn't I think of that while I was in the shop? I didn't relish the prospect of going back there alone, not after the icy finale to this morning's shopping. It seemed more than a little ironic that I was now treated as the enemy by *both* sides in this Highland cold war. Ah well, the letter would just have to wait until I plucked up sufficient courage or thought of some other way round the problem.

One immediate temporary solution was provided by what I thought of as a remarkably cunning ploy. I added to the already numerous blots on the page by placing another carefully over the beginning of the date. This meant that as long as the letter was posted by the end of the month, then it would still appear fairly recent. Any further delays could be dealt with by means of a bigger blot. With that problem settled I made a few attempts at addressing the envelope. Once I had come up with a reasonably legible version I licked the bitter gum on the flap of the envelope and stuck it in place.

Laying the letter aside I began to experiment with the pen. It was possible to write very small by holding the nib the wrong way up, at least until the ink stopped flowing or a hole was scratched through the paper. I practised writing my name, at first indulging in a few debonair signatures, but finally settling for a print as neat as I could manage. Father had given me the pen with my name engraved in the metal of the barrel. Perhaps he had written with a similar pen. I opened the notorious bird book to compare our two signatures. His looked far neater than mine, but then, you've had so much more practice by the time you're twelve.

From these innocent comparisons I allowed myself to slip once more onto a see-saw of darker speculation. How much did my father really know about Henry when he ordered me to be passed into his clutches? Just when I had succeeded in absolving him from most of the blame by employing a few convenient assumptions, new evidence had presented itself. Last night, at supper, I had heard Henry use one of Father's catch-phrases. Either that or . . . But surely not. Father couldn't have picked it up from Henry. Could he? I began to worry. My suspicions were once more well and truly aroused. It was not a phrase that I had heard anywhere else. Nor was it one that Father had used lightly, as it represented his own personal philosophy of the kitchen. I quelled the phantom of fried potato, which did nothing for Father's case, before continuing along this line of thought. Could it be that Father had not only spent some time here, but had been here long enough to pick up this phrase and even the way of thinking that was behind it? It seemed impossible, and yet very difficult to explain otherwise. If he had been here that long, then he would surely have known what Henry was like and . . .

I was not aided in this internal inquiry by the distinct lack of information that Father had provided about his own past. Most of the tales he told were either bizarre creations or truths embellished with the kind of colourful exaggerations that entertain the child by teasing his credulity. Sadly, he had died before these fictional decorations had time to be replaced by the less amusing truth which my later years would demand. Without any guide to help sort them out they were inclined to twist in my mind into lies, which in turn cast doubt over all the other stories, no matter how true or innocently intended they may have been. And so I was left sitting at that desk with few clues to help me avoid the conclusions which pressed in upon me. That is, until I was rescued by a swift comparison, so useful in re-shaping unpalatable truths. I thought carefully about these two men. There was Father, the workaholic idealist. And there was Henry who was, well, just Henry. There was no way that the two of them could share the same side of the scales. I was being quite ridiculous. In no way could the Henry that I knew have influenced the way that Father thought, they were quite plainly too different. There had to be some other explanation and I soon thought of one that seemed to fit the evidence, whilst still allowing me to draw the conclusions that I wanted to draw. The answer was that Father *had* spent some time here, there was no way I could deny it, but that Henry, since then, had quite obviously changed. Father, only remembering the Henry of old, had sent me here in good faith. He was absolved, Henry was partly let off as something dreadful must have brought about the change, and I had assured myself that no one really wanted to do me any harm. I mean, how could they?

I sat back, satisfied as much by the ingenuity of my explanation as by the conclusion I had reached. I felt so much happier now. But then, ignorance is bliss, and I was, as usual, completely wrong.

fourteen

*In which the outside world has
some contact with me*

I did not sleep too well that night. The usual post-supper security of my room had been disturbed by the unexpected appearance of Henry. Having once more absolved Father from any blame, it was now permissible to miss him again so, feeling a little sad, I lay on the bed, staring at the ceiling in a reverie of fragile thought. The door opened suddenly and in stepped Henry, holding, at arms length, my trousers.

'I thought it wise to bring these in before a dew falls and wets them again.'

'Thank you,' I replied, sitting up.

'Should you ever wish to launder your clothes whilst *not* wearing them, there are facilities to do so.'

He dropped the trousers into my lap, then looked past me to where the bear sat on the pillow. I prayed that he would go away and leave us alone but instead he reached over and picked Bear up by his ear.

'Hmm,' he snorted. 'I suppose this could explain a lot. If people will give impressionable children toys which exhibit the worst characteristics of both men and beasts, is it surprising that they grow up the way they do? Though I'm probably being unfair. They would no doubt end up that way anyway.' He tossed Bear back onto the bed, where he lay with one paw raised in what I liked to think of as an obscene gesture of defiance. I hoped that Henry's latest little sermon on the follies of man might mark the end of his visit, but no, he ambled over to the desk, examined one of my drawings with his head set on one side, then proceeded to stare out of the window in silence.

'This should provide a splendid view when the time comes.' He said at last.

'When what time comes?'

'The war, of course.' He replied impatiently. 'We should be just far enough away from where the bombs fall to see it all go up, before we too are blown into blissful oblivion with the rest of this blighted planet.' He turned with a smile. 'I suppose that's one thing to be said for stuffed bears. At least they don't breed. Your parents were good that way too. Once they had made their own contribution to world over-population they at least had the decency to balance it out with a swift and early demise. A course of action which should soon be increasing no end in popularity.' He smiled all the more at this and, having cheered himself up with this little joke, said a curt goodnight and was gone as quickly as he had come.

It is not easy to sleep after an encounter like that. In addition to being upset at the things he had said about my parents, and the bear, the thought crossed my mind that Henry might feel the need to start purging the world of humanity single-handed. Starting in the night with me. This absurd thought troubled me enough to get out of bed and prop a chair against the door, just in case, an action which caused no end of panic and confusion when I stumbled over it in the dark on the way to the toilet.

Despite my stringent security measures it was still some time before I finally nodded off and I was tired enough in the morning to sleep through all but the final and most strident burblings of the boiler, wakening with only just enough time to wash and dress. Breakfast passed without any further apocalyptic prophecies, or any conversation for that matter, and I returned to my room unscathed.

Daylight had removed the worst of any fears I might have had about Henry's potentially murderous nature, but his dark words and gruesome jokes stayed with me. Henry was most alarming when you stopped and thought not just about what he said, but why he said it. There were, to my mind, two possible explanations for the dreadful things that he said. It could be that he deliberately set out to shock and offend, which indicated a most unpleasant character. On the other hand, perhaps the shock and offence were merely side effects. Maybe Henry was simply very honest. Perhaps he just said exactly what he thought. If the first possibility was worrying, the second was terrifying, and something told me that it was the more frightening of the two that was the closest to the truth.

Still, I had to keep my spirits up. The only thing to do was spend as little time as possible in the house, and thus avoid Henry as much as I could. Out came the map. I had not thought of exploring the area beyond the loch, or the woods that hung on the hillside above the village. The land around the road that led in to the glen was still a mystery. There was much to see and do; I had a chance to wander and play in some of the most glorious scenery in the land, so I must not grow downhearted. Father used to quote a motto, in Latin, which he said was about not letting certain people grind you down. Well, I wouldn't. I was going to enjoy myself in spite of Henry, starting today with some serious exploring. I pored over the map, comparing what I read with the surrounding countryside, trying to match the lines and colours to the hills outside. It was while I was comparing the map version with the real road up to the house that I first saw the figure coming up the hill. I blinked and looked again. Who in their right mind would be coming to visit Henry? It couldn't be the post man, because he drove a Land Rover. Whoever it was seemed to be making heavy weather of the steeper parts of the road. He vanished from sight then reappeared by the hedge. As he turned into the drive I could see that it was a small, thin man wearing an ecclesiastical dog collar. This was odd. Perhaps he had come to exorcise the evil spirit of Henry. I found this quite funny until I thought that perhaps the villagers *had* thought me possessed. (This may have been a wild assumption, but it wasn't all that far from the truth.)

Whatever he had come for he couldn't get on with it until someone opened the door. He tried the heavy knocker again. No sign of life downstairs. Out of the back window I could see Henry down in the garden, busy with his vegetables and oblivious to the knocking. I ran down both flights of stairs and into the hall. There I hesitated before the front door, unsure of whether to open it or not. In the end I decided to leave it and call Henry.

'Henry. Henry?' I called timidly. He didn't hear. I ran up the lawn. 'Henry?'

'Yes, boy?' He didn't look up.

'There's someone at the door.' Henry stood up and turned around. 'Not now there isn't,' he said.

I looked round to see the figure advancing purposefully across the lawn towards us.

'Well, well,' said Henry slowly, with a worrying smile, 'if it isn't Monsignor Murchie, the parish priest.' The Reverend Murchie, of the Church of Scotland, looked rather upset by this insult to his religious proclivities, but seemed too inflated by his sense of purpose to rise to Henry's bait.

'Henry Dundas,' he said over my head in a dull, nasal voice, 'I have reason to believe that you have a child living here with you.'

'Really? What makes you think that?' Henry asked incredulously. The minister almost began to point towards me but recoiled his finger before he could look too stupid.

'Mr Graham in the shop told me that a wee boy had come in claiming to be your nephew.'

'Claiming?' said Henry. 'He *is* my nephew. And anyway, Murchie, is there some parish law which bans my family from shopping?'

'*Reverend* Murchie, if you don't mind,' he protested.

'Well I do mind, Murchie. I mind having you within a mile of my house. I mind having your unsavoury bigoted little personage on my lawn, and I mind you coming up here and sticking your weasely little nose in where it is not required.'

'As minister of this parish I felt it my duty to enquire about the boy's spiritual welfare.'

Henry laughed. 'And what do you know of the spirit Murchie? Apart from the cheap whisky you pour down your throat in the Stag after rendering your priggish congregation semi-comatose with one of your incoherent sermons.' I could tell that Henry didn't like him. The minister struggled to sustain his righteous momentum.

'And I was also concerned about his physical welfare. Mr Graham said that the boy bought two large bars of chocolate, and doubted if he was being properly fed.'

'Show Murchie your protruding ribs, boy. Then, once he has admired your rickets he can go back to the village and round up a rescue party.' I fumbled vaguely at my shirt. 'Oh for goodness sake, boy,' muttered Henry, and I gathered that it had not been intended seriously. Henry turned to the minister. 'Now then, Murchie. Why don't you run along back to your flock and tend to their "spiritual needs" in the final hours before Armageddon?'

'I'm not leaving until I have spoken to the boy.'

Henry sighed. 'Talk to Murchie, boy. Let him die happy.' He turned back to his vegetables and left me with the Reverend, who switched automatically into a kindly mode.

'Now you must understand that I don't mean to upset your uncle. It's just that I was surprised to hear that there was a wee boy living up here. Mind you, you're not so wee, are you?' he laughed. I remained unimpressed. Cautiously he tried again. 'Well, as I said, I was a bit surprised to find out that you were here, given that your uncle is . . . that is, that he has something of a reputation for . . . well, you know what I mean.' Nodding in Henry's direction he smiled conspiratorially.

'No,' I replied, looking deliberately puzzled.

'Ah, yes, well of course . . .' he stammered, then tried another, equally slimy, tack.

'I'm sure that everything's just fine, but I just wanted to check. You see, we have a nice Sunday school which we hold at the manse on . . .'

'Sundays?' I volunteered brightly.

'Yes, that's right,' he answered sycophantically. If sarcasm was the lowest form of wit it was still aimed too high in his case. But I

83

was still enjoying myself. Here was a chance to avenge myself on the church for the violence of my unwanted baptism. With no headmaster to be sent to either.

'Well, I was thinking that maybe . . . you must get awful lonely up here.'

'No.' There followed a squirming silence.

'No, of course not. But perhaps you would like to meet some of the other wee . . .'

'Not really. I like being by myself.' As well as adding to the minister's awkwardness, this statement was perfectly true. I had always been a bit of a loner.

'Oh well. But we will see you in the kirk of course. You are a member of the church, aren't you?'

'No.'

The veneer of charm began to peel a little . . .

'You're not a Catholic, are you?'

'No. I'm not anything. I don't really believe in God and I don't want to go to church or Sunday school. I'm quite happy just where I am, thank you.'

Once again I had found myself on the Henry side of this war of nerves, though not through any great sense of loyalty. Even to a ten-year-old the Reverend Murchie's motives were transparently clear. My welfare didn't come into it. All he wanted was one small admission, one little clue to indicate that this time Henry had gone too far. I was being used as a pawn in a game whose sole object was to find some concrete evidence that would finally condemn Henry. I was to provide that evidence. But I wasn't having any of it. There was a lot I would have liked to say about Henry, but not to this ferrety little man. I made my stubborn point and his face fell. The smile and the jolly tone evaporated. Puffing out what little chest he had the Reverend walked past me as if I had just vanished into thin air, and addressed Henry with loud indignation.

'I don't know what you have done to this boy, Henry Dundas, but mark my words, you haven't heard the last of it.'

Henry rose wearily from his weeding. He ambled over to the little minister, over whom he towered by many inches, and smiled one of his patient smiles. The kind of smile that would bring your teeth out in a cold sweat. He brought his face close to Murchie's. Murchie retreated from the neck up, like a tortoise withdrawing into its dog collar. Henry's voice was so quiet and gentle that it scared the wits out of me and I was several yards away.

'Go away,' he intoned carefully, 'and don't come back.' Then, taking the frozen pastor by the shoulders he rotated him through 180 degrees.

'That is the way out. Goodbye, Murchie.'

The minister tried to walk away with what little dignity he still had left. He was about to round the corner of the house when Henry called out to him.

'By the way, Murchie. A word of comfort for your parishioners in their final hours. I've heard that in the event of war the Pope is to grant a special dispensation, so that even Presbyterians will be allowed into Hell.'

Henry's laughter speeded the minister's departure and he turned to me, still smiling.

'Well, boy. You obviously didn't say whatever Murchie wanted to hear.'

I didn't like the way that he sounded so pleased with himself. If I wasn't going to be used by one side then the same applied to Henry. Adrenalin still coursed around me from my encounter with the Minister and, on the rash spur of the moment, I stated my independence.

'I just told him the truth.' My courage peaked. 'And it had nothing to do with you.' I turned sharply on my heels and marched indoors. Then ran like hell up the stairs, slamming the bedroom door behind me. I stood with my back to it as the courage and colour drained from my face. My God. What had I said?!

fifteen

❧

*In which there is much fear and
loathing in the attic*

I remained with my back to that door for some time, listening for
the inevitable sound of angry footsteps coming up the stairs, intent
on punishing me for my insolence. I had given myself quite a
shock. As much by having spoken at all as by what I had said. In
the context of my usual silence, anything said to Henry took on
dreadful importance, and I was alarmed enough to think that my
words had had the same effect on him as they were now having on
me. So I stood there, tensed against the door, heart beating
desperately as it tried to get out of my rib-cage and off to
somewhere safer. Several minutes passed. Still no sound from
below. In a suitable gesture of temporary relief I allowed my eyes to
close and my head to loll back, catching myself a nasty knock with
the bottom of the coat-hook which made me start away from the
door. It was probably for the best. Henry could move about the
house very quietly and any second now an axe might crash through
the white wooden panels, making a nasty tear in my dressing-gown.
But it didn't.

I crept across the room to the back window, cautiously peering
round the curtain at the garden below. There was Henry, seemingly
still intent on weeding his vegetable patch. But he knew that he was

being watched, for he straightened slightly and rubbed at the small of his back before continuing in the same ordinary way. He wasn't fooling anyone. I knew that he was toying with me, as Oscar would with a mouse. If he ever caught one. I moved back from the window. There was no way out except by going downstairs. Where he would be waiting. I was trapped.

I did think of flashing an SOS out of the window with my torch. But only the villagers would be able to see it, and they thought me part of the Henry camp. Besides, the signal would not be helped by the copious amounts of broad daylight that pervaded the glen. There I was, just like David Balfour in *Kidnapped*, with an evil uncle plotting my demise and the authorities accusing me of a crime which I hadn't committed. How did he get out of it? He fled to the hills, as must I. I would hide in the high and lonely places, live on nuts and berries, clubbing the occasional grouse for variety. I peeked out of the window again. No Henry! A bit more door-leaning. Still no sound. I must take a chance and run for it. I grabbed the first aids to escape that came to mind and hand, the torch and the chocolate. And, of course, the map. I opened the door with the delicacy of a surgeon. Silence from below. Down the stairs, checking on the landing for any signs of life. From the study came the sound of the wireless. That should cover my escape. One by one by one down the second flight, each step a thousand prayers long. Can't risk passing the study, so try the front door with its Yale and mortice locks.

I fumbled with the key and the latch, turning both and managing to open the Yale while locking the mortice. Reverse the process, undoing the mortice and re-locking the Yale. Undo the Yale and then pull. It won't budge. Further panic as I turn the key and once more lock the mortice. Turn it back and pull. Pull harder. Harder! Then, an idea. Try turning the door knob. Pulling too hard in my frenzy I toppled over, sandwiching myself between the door and wall, knocking down the brolly stand with a clatter. I stopped with natural politeness to pick it up before remembering the urgency of my escape. I barely managed to avoid measuring my length on the gravel as I tripped over the mat and flew out into the drive, skidded round the corner and sprinted off up the hill path. I didn't stop until I reached a copse of stunted trees and crouched there, sheltering amongst the grey twisted limbs. There was no sign of pursuit, so I began to move again, climbing up towards the horizon.

I think it was when my shoe came off in the boggy bit on the ridge that I first doubted the wisdom of my decision. There was an unholy slurp as I hauled my foot free to find it clad only in a sock. It took a great deal of one-legged balancing to retrieve the shoe from the mud. I did my best to avoid sticking my sock into the slimy ground but still managed to acquire an extra lining to my shoe when it was finally pulled onto dry land. I continued on my way in a rather more sober frame of mind. This sudden intrusion of the world in its squelchy reality had succeeded in knocking some of the paranoia out of my sails. Perhaps I was being a little hasty. But then again . . . I thought carefully about Henry as I walked on. We were dealing here with a man who, for some dark reason, was reviled by all who knew him, and who said the most unpleasant and shocking things to anyone and everyone, even going so far as to verbally abuse and physically man-handle men of the cloth. Perhaps this isn't such a stupid idea after all. A man who behaves like that is capable of anything. I walked on, newly determined.

I was following the ridge that ran from the hill behind the house up to meet the other side of the valley at the head of the glen, high above the tapering end of the loch. The loch looked blue from up here, still free from the shadow of the cloud that crept over from my left, above the miniature glen that dipped before rising to the full height of the mountain. It was on the other side of this little dale that I first saw a movement. A brown shape moved across the heather. Then another, until I realised that I was watching a large herd of red deer browsing across the face of the mountain. I watched them as I walked on, now taking extra care to look out for other signs of life. It was like being handed a key that opened up the secret world of the hills. Soon I began to spot numerous birds and animals. Rabbits ran off as I approached and brown butterflies flickered over the heather. The deer still moved steadily across the hill side and with them drifted the shadows of clouds. The clouds grew darker and heavier until the sun itself had disappeared, turning much of the green to grey and lifting most of the warmth from the air.

This chill made me stop and wonder if perhaps I was heading in the wrong direction given that civilisation, i.e. the world outside the glen, lay the other way. I opened the map and crouched over it to see if an about turn was in order. I calculated that once I reached the head of the glen it would be possible to climb down the other side. Then, after following this burn to its source here, there was only a small hill to climb before a path wound down this other glen to meet the Inverness road. It was as simple as that – a matter of a mere thirty miles or so. I ate some chocolate, always a marvellous source of renewed optimism, and decided that this was what I would do. By travelling across country I would be impossible to trace. What I would do once I had reached the road I wasn't quite sure, but one can only do so much planning at any one time. I would burn that bridge when I came to it. The map was folded away, the chocolate folded away in its wrapper with remarkable self-discipline, and the journey continued in earnest.

As the ridge rose the sheep track began to peter out, giving way to heather and more boggy patches, fragrant with myrtle, which I skirted with as much caution as the adder-infested bracken. The heather made for heavy going, clinging to the wool of my socks and tugging at my shoe laces. After walking for what seemed like hours, and most probably was, I seemed to be no nearer to the head of the glen, which just stayed stubbornly where it was, as the moon follows a speeding train. What I had managed to reach was a deep crevice, cut into the hillside by a fast burn which tumbled down towards the floor of the glen. This gap was too wide to be jumped. I would have to find a way round it.

I turned off to the left. Where there was heather it grew thicker, where there wasn't the ground grew even marshier. The sky grew blacker, and this crack in the ground grew longer and wider the more I followed it. I was sure that there must be some place where I could cross. All the map showed was a little blue line, but then maps, even ones that I have folded, are so deceptively flat, and several hundred crows could have flown the distance and back in the time it took me to struggle and leap through bog and bracken. All I seemed to be doing was taking myself further away from my intended route and my target of the head of the glen, which seemed happy to recede far faster than it would ever approach. And then water conspired to attack from all sides. I stepped with both feet on to a tussock which wasn't and sank past my ankles. I had just managed to extricate myself when the first cold drops of rain began to fall. It was becoming harder and harder to justify this expedition, even on the severely watered-down grounds of allowing Henry time to cool off. His psychopathic tendencies had been abandoned way back on the ridge.

Nor were my imaginings the only thing to be watered down. I was now soaking wet. I had brought no waterproof and my jumper and shirt clung to my skin. I was starting to feel frightened as every square inch of ground seemed to soften into one great bog. I finally conceded that I couldn't go on like this: I would have to go back. The sky was growing darker and, besides, it was nearly suppertime. Henry really would be angry if I was late. What was I doing here anyway? Why should he want to harm me if he's so sure that we have so little time left? It wouldn't be worth the effort. Father would never have sent me here if he had thought that I might come to harm. I had to go back. Everything was grey and black, no hilltops to be seen as the rain sheeted across the glen as if to sweep me away. The ground was sinking beneath my feet. I began to run towards the path as if speed would carry me over this phantom ground. Sinking again, almost screaming in panic, the rain heavier and heavier, then tripping to fall face first into sharp wet heather. Pulling myself up, a cut on my hand, rain in my eyes, tears on my face. Scrambling up onto the ridge and beginning to stumble along the slippery path. Lights in the village so very far below. Tripping through more heather, then heart stopping dead as a black demon of a grouse goes whirring up from beneath my very feet. Terrified and weeping I stopped in my tracks, noticing that several extra miles of ridge had crept up behind me on the outward journey and now formed an endless path back to the house. Wherever that was. I had no idea which path led back to the house, which path might just take me over a cliff. I stumbled on along the ridge, unsure of what I was doing when something bright yellow stood out from the colourless atmosphere. It was coming towards me and slowly transforming itself into a great oilskin cape and sou'wester. It shouted at me through the rain.

'There you are, boy. What in God's name are you doing up here in this weather, you cretinous child?'

I stopped and stared, my numb hands gripping the limp bundle of sodden map and dissolving chocolate.

'Hurry up, boy. Don't just stand there,' said the yellow Henry as it reached me. He grabbed my hand and began to march me down a path, feet barely touching the ground, down towards the house.

'You seem to have a strange affinity for water. That, and your general stupidity, must have been inherited from your father. He was always getting himself wet in one way or another.'

I was unceremoniously dragged into the lobby. Henry stopped to close the door against the rain before removing his waterproofs. Stepping out of his wellingtons he turned to me, as I stood dripping vacantly, and said 'Wait here.' I waited, and dripped vacantly a little more. He returned after a minute with a huge white towel.

'Remove all that wet clothing and leave it here. Do not drip on my carpets. Go upstairs. I had the foresight to switch on the boiler and have run a bath for you. Get into it, wash, thaw out, ponder your stupidity, dry yourself, dress, then be down in the kitchen in half an hour. Supper is already extremely overdue.'

I obeyed without word or thought, climbing the stairs in bare feet and towel to the mocking gurgle of the plumbing. The bath was gloriously hot and long with big brass taps at the end and a plug and chain of marine anchor proportions. There was a yellow bar of coal tar soap, a loofah, a most intriguing antique back brush and a sponge, all sitting in a rack across the bath. I sank back in the steam feeling extremely foolish and sure that I was in for a severe reprimand. But right now I didn't care. To be off that hill, and in the warm as the rain battered against the window, was enough. I lay back to enjoy what was left of the half hour.

I dressed in my room, putting on a pair of warm corduroy trousers, a fresh shirt and a heavy pullover. I even combed my wet hair and wished that the warm post bath sensation extended below my skin to my stomach, where a miniature version of this afternoon's storm seemed to be taking place. It churned away at the thought of what lay downstairs.

When I arrived in the kitchen it was distracted momentarily from its churning by the delicious smells which filled the room. Henry was at the cooker, stirring a vast cauldron of a pan. He did not turn round as he spoke.

'Sit down, boy.' I sat. 'Man has no mastery over those hills. They can put him in his place whenever they wish to do so. That is part of their charm. It is also why it is so unutterably moronic for anyone to go up there without being properly prepared. The ground is treacherously marshy and the weather can turn almost Arctic, even in the middle of summer. Those hills can be, and often have been, fatal. For this reason I would be grateful if you would not disappear into them without knowing what you are doing, and thus refrain from asserting your mortality before the rest of us. Your unexplained death would only lead to me being further pestered by the Murchies of this world and their officious ilk. They would no doubt make an awful fuss.'

He came over to the table with a round bread board, upon which sat a fresh baked loaf, still pervading the air with its warm scent. The soup was served up and Henry sat down.

'Still, youth is prone to wander. But that is not the place to do so.' He began to eat. 'Yes. We must do something about that,' he added ominously.

There was not another word spoken during the course of the meal. As I buttered my bread and ate the soup I worried about this closing remark. Did he plan, perhaps, to amputate my legs to stop me from wandering? No, don't be daft. There I was, allowing head-room to the same kind of absurd thought that had landed me in this predicament in the first place. No, of course not. He would probably just chain me to a tree.

sixteen

❧

In which I am confined to quarters

As it transpired there was no need for manacles as I had successfully grounded myself. During the night I was sure that a volcano was erupting and that poisonous fumes were slowly choking me to death . . . . I sat up to find that my respiratory system was in the same ruinous state as the plumbing and that both were producing an inordinate amount of noise. Either the boiler was getting worse or the sound just carried more at night, but whatever the reason its gurglings, and my sniffings, wheezings and coughings, were conspiring to keep me awake.

I heaved myself out of bed and walked quietly downstairs to the toilet where I gathered a handful of paper with which to blow my nose. From the landing window I could see the garden, wet after the rain, turning to silver under the light of the moon. All very poetic, but it looked as cold and miserable as I felt, so I shuffled back upstairs to honk hopelessly into the paper and feel feverishly sorry for myself.

I woke the next morning feeling as if I was wearing a balaclava on the inside of my head. Every joint ached, and it is a measure of just how dire I felt that I even ignored my watch as it ticked past the breakfast hour. Such flagrant unpunctuality could not go unnoticed for long and, right enough, at fourteen minutes past eight the door opened to reveal Henry. He stood at the foot of the bed while I pretended not to have noticed. I hoped that he might go away again but, when I realised that he wouldn't, I took advantage of a passing sneezing fit to feign waking suddenly from a deep and fevered sleep.

'Oh gosh! Am I late?' I cried, adding to the effect by treating Henry to one of my lung-racking coughs.

'Pneumonia is it, boy?' I groaned and tried to sit up, wheezing all the way.

'There's no need to overdo it. I have been able to hear enough of your revolting catarrhal eruptions from downstairs to be convinced of your ill-health. Hardly surprising given your oafish behaviour of yesterday. Well, you can jolly well stay just where you are. I'm not having you spreading your vile bacteria around my kitchen.'

Henry sighed, shook his head and left. Is that it? No breakfast or anything? Obviously he believes in starving both colds and fevers. Oh well, I'm sure that I'll get by. Besides, I don't feel like doing much except sleeping. I must have dozed off again for a while and was aroused by the sound of someone struggling with the door. It was Henry, having trouble opening the door while also carrying a tray. On the tray was a boiled egg, some toast and a large glass of orange juice.

'Vitamin C,' said Henry, 'invaluable in the treatment of colds.' He picked the bear off the bedside chair by his frayed ear and dropped him on the floor with a look of disgust. The tray was set beside me as I embarked on yet another bout of coughing, in an attempt to somehow justify the invalid treatment.

'Oh do try to die quietly, boy,' were Henry's only other words before he left the room.

I managed to summon up the strength to sit up and eat breakfast, before settling down to a good long languish. It was a languish which was to last for several days, and not solely by design. I did feel thoroughly rotten and really quite feverish, dividing my days between short bursts of reading and long bursts of sleeping. Henry appeared at regular intervals with light meals and copious amounts of life-giving orange juice. These visits were usually as silent as normal meals, although punctuated by the occasional remark about just how revolting the sounds that I was making really were.

The following day I was definitely feeling worse. Positively tubercular in fact. It was all very well injecting the seniors at school, but what about us poor primary lads, left to die a slow consumptive death? In my more lucid moments, when death did not rap so loudly on the door of my fading existence, I managed to pick my way through the rest of *Kidnapped*, leaving David Balfour, who always managed to escape across the hills from his enemies without catching double pneumonia and being hauled home for a bath, enjoying the prospect of his inheritance. It's all right for some. All I had to look foward to was what remained of my chocolate and the prospect of a war in which I would most definitely not have the chance to buckle my swash against fiendish, but none the less chivalrous, enemies. I decided to sleep some more and noted a definite decline in my condition when Henry prodded me awake for a supper of soup and bread.

Another fitful night of sleep and coughing took me through to Monday morning, when I was most disappointed to find that it was once more possible to breath without sounding like the more dramatic sort of desert wind. However, it doesn't do to rush these things and risk a relapse, so I remained quite firmly where I was. I tried not to disappoint Henry with this sudden recuperation by continuing to hack and wheeze away in the same manner as before, but he seemed strangely attuned to the true state of my well-being.

'I trust that you are not going to remain in bed indefinitely. I think you should be passable as wholesome enough to re-enter the kitchen by tomorrow. You can't go on just lying there, boy. You are young! You have your whole life in front of you,' he announced grandly, 'and that is not a fortnight you should squander lightly.'

Henry found this very funny indeed and departed sniggering to himself. I remained unamused and lay back to make the most of my last bed-ridden day. Unfortunately, I was growing rather bored by this time. I found it hard to summon up the energy to be ill any more so reluctantly sidled out of bed and over to the window. The weather seemed to be quite reasonable, but not spectacular enough to justify a full blown recovery, though I did decide to extend my languish beyond the bed to other parts of the room, but no further than that. And certainly not as far as actually getting dressed.

I passed the rest of the day in my dressing-gown, pottering about the desk, playing patience for a while and doing the easy bits of a jigsaw before growing bored with the umpteen identical bits in the dark green corner. I picked up the letter for Margaret, which had still not seen the business end of a post box, and wondered if I should open it and add some more blots before I ran out of July. In the end I settled on leaving it safely in the envelope and determining to find some way of getting it into the post before too long. But that was easier said than done.

seventeen

❦

*In which Henry has more contact with the
outside world than it could ever want.*

The following morning I was forced to admit that I felt a good deal
better. Still a bit of a runny nose, but no more death's-door
wheezing or coughing. It did not seem wise to stretch Henry's
patience by attempting yet another day in bed, so I dutifully rose to
the sound of the boiler and dressed in plenty of time for breakfast.
When I arrived in the kitchen Henry had just finished feeding
Oscar. He closed the lobby door and turned to where I sat at the
table.

'Ah! So Lazarus is risen. I trust that you are feeling in more
robust health than before?'

'Yes, thank you.'

'Good, because I have a plan for today which is designed to kill
several birds with one stone.' He served up breakfast as I visualised
the rolling of a huge boulder onto the chicken coop. On aesthetic
grounds.

'Your presence here has disrupted my living cycle more than a
little. I have supplies delivered from an establishment in Inverness
once a month. I make a visit there to place an order and at the same
time, by seeing humanity in relatively large numbers, reassure
myself of the pleasures of living in solitude. Or, rather, the

pleasures of solitude that once were.' He looked pointedly at me. I tried to look apologetic, but he had already continued. 'Having another mouth to feed has depleted supplies somewhat. Especially that of fruit juice, which you have single-handedly demolished over the course of the weekend. Being a creature of habit I do not intend changing the time of my visit, which does not fall for a fortnight or so. This means that the larder must be topped up by means of a visit to Graham's wretched emporium in the village. I believe you have already had the misfortune of doing business with him.'

'Yes. I have.'

'This trip will allow me to achieve several things at the same time, especially if you will be so good as to accompany me. Assuming that is that you are now sufficiently healthy?'

The gory absence of several limbs would not have constituted sufficient grounds for me to decline Henry's offer. I nodded earnestly.

'Good. If you come with me then not only will I have an extra pair of hands available for the carrying of provisions, but it will also allow you the chance to take some exercise which does not result in a slow death by exposure and at the same time assure the good people of the village that you have not met an untimely end. Not that I value their opinions in the least, but I will lower myself to pander this much in the hope that it will guarantee my freedom from further visits by the likes of Murchie.'

Henry produced his watch and consulted it at length as if working something out.

'Allowing time for the drawing up of lists and so on I think that we shall be ready to depart at about nine thirty.'

'Yes. That would be fine,' I concurred. Henry looked up in a way that told me that my approval was neither here nor there. Breakfast concluded in silence and I went up to my room to prepare.

I had little choice about going shopping with Henry, an absurd enough concept in itself, but at the same time it did happen to solve the problem of the letter. I would now be able to post it without the fear of entering the shop alone. I did not imagine that Henry's company would make me any more welcome in the shop, but I reckoned that I would not feel quite so nervous with Henry riding shotgun. Especially now that some degree of childhood security had once more been restored to my life. Freedom to do just what you want may well be the child's dream but, over the last few days, I had been told what to do, when to have a bath, what and when to eat and when to stay in bed. Even Henry's manner could not detract from the comfort that this authority had secretly brought. So perhaps that was why I did not feel quite the amount of trepidation that might have been expected when I made my way downstairs at the appointed hour.

Henry was just outside the lobby, inspecting the plum trees which hung over the coal bunker. Oscar lay stretched out across the lid, paralysed by a sunbeam.

'Ah, there you are, boy,' said Henry and handed me the smaller of two canvas grips. The day still had a bit of a chill about it as we set off down the hill, although the sun was already well established in a sky of almost autumnal height and crispness. My nose, now almost its old functional self, was refreshed by the mingling scents of bracken and pine, the distinctive perfume of this rugged country. Down we strode, Henry at his usual marching pace and me struggling to keep up. A rabbit shot across the road and vanished into the trees as we approached the bridge. Here Henry paused for a while, watching the waters of the burn pass below in an earnest gurgle of private conversation. It was just before we reached the kirk, at the point where the main road enters the village, that something most peculiar happened. We were walking along the right hand side of the road and had just come to the junction when a Land Rover passed us round the corner. From its open window a hand extended in a static wave and a voice cried cheerily –

'Hello there, Henry. Grand morning isn't it?'

Henry waved back with a dismissive gesture and the voice changed gear and laughed its way up the hill until it vanished from sight. Henry seemed quite unperturbed but I was, to say the least, astonished. I stood staring after this remarkable stranger who had dared to greet Henry in this cheery fashion. After several yards Henry noticed that I was no longer in step and called back impatiently.

'Good Lord, boy, surely you haven't been away from the modern world so long that you can be astonished by the internal combustion engine? Stop gawping and hurry up.'

I hurried, but it took a little longer to undo the gawp.

'Just wait until we get to the village,' added Henry. 'They have electricity there.' Like a fool I rose to his teasing and tried to defend myself.

'It wasn't that, I just . . . '

'Yes?'

'I was just wondering . . . '

'Who the excessively jolly cretin in the Land Rover was?'

'Well, yes,' I admitted quietly.

'That, boy, is MacIntyre, the village quack. He's nearly as old as I am, God help him, so should have retired years ago. Still, at least he'll soon have senility as a valid excuse for his incompetence. With the honourable exception of the apocalypse itself he is probably the greatest single threat to human health that there is.'

And, I thought, the only person whom I had ever seen treating Henry with something other than fear or disgust. But Henry elaborated no further, so I was none the wiser when we turned into the main street. Up the pavement we walked abreast like a pair of gunfighters, gossiping neighbours disappearing into doorways and net curtains twitching on every side.

Only those trapped inside the shop were unable to dodge the coming of Henry. We reached the postcards of the door. The pink draylon headboard (2'6") had still not been sold. The bell rang. Seconds out, round one. Henry stepped inside to the roar of silence. All eyes turned to him and he slowly acknowledged each pair with his calm gaze, turning every one of them back to the counter. Only Graham, the shop-keeper, was left facing outwards.

'I have an idea, Graham,' Henry said suddenly, causing a slight jump around the row of silent backs. 'Why don't you install a Western style honky-tonk piano in that corner, and employ someone whose sole purpose would be to stop playing as soon as I enter this shabby little establishment. I do so feel that it would add no end to the fun and suspense.'

Graham pretended not to hear and spoke to a nearby customer.

'I'll just have a look for you through the back, Mrs Donald. I think we might have one there.' Mrs Donald looked rather puzzled, as if she hadn't even asked for one, whatever it was, but now felt obliged to wait for Graham to come back with it, just in case.

Henry ambled over to the shelves of groceries leaving me, who had been sheltering behind him, exposed. Everyone looked at me. I shuffled sideways and joined Henry. He was working his way down the list, gathering whatever he needed and shuttling backwards and forwards leaving a pile on the counter. It was soon complete and Henry stood waiting to pay for his groceries next to Mrs Donald, who was still wondering if she needed one. Graham still hadn't managed to find it, but was obviously determined to keep up the search as long as Henry was in the shop. This left the counter unattended. Mrs Graham was busy with the post office section, Graham wasn't going to come out so that left their unfortunate teenage daughter, who was pushed out from the back looking worried and embarrassed. She stood smiling vacantly for a while. Henry smiled back.

'I would like to pay for this small heap of victuals, if that's not too inconvenient,' he said.

'Yes, of course.' She began to add up the total on a piece of paper, finally announcing the sum after much pencil-chewing.

'Assuming that you are using the same arithmetical axioms as the rest of us,' Henry said, 'you have erred by some twenty five per cent in my favour.'

'Oh dear. Have I?' She added again. 'Oh yes. I have. Sorry. I don't know what's wrong with me.'

'Several generations of in-breeding, I should imagine. Don't worry, it's quite common in these parts,' Henry assured her.

Once the sum had finally been settled Henry paid up and began to fill the canvas bag. I took what I thought to be a reasonable share of the load and followed Henry out of the shop. The door had just closed behind us when I remembered why I had come in the first place.

'Stamps.'

'I beg your pardon?' said Henry.

'I've forgotten to get the stamps.'

'Well do hurry up.'

I pushed the door open and rushed into the shop, just as Graham reappeared behind the counter. He checked carefully that I was Henryless before staying.

'Did you find it?' asked Mrs Donald.

'Find what?'

'You know. The er . . . through the back, did you have one?'

'Ah, yes. No, I'm afraid that I didn't. But maybe next week.' He was too busy watching me, keeping the other eye on Henry who hovered outside the door. I walked nervously up to the post office counter. Graham moved quickly round to the other side of it.

'I'll deal with this, dear,' he said quietly to his wife. She nodded conspiratorially and disappeared into the back of the shop.

'I'd like a first-class stamp, please.'

'Certainly,' came the cheery reply. This was not what I had been expecting. 'Posting a letter are you?' He was friendliness itself.

'Yes, that's right,' I replied, wondering what else you could do with a first-class stamp.

'Good good. Now then, let's find you a nice stamp.' The door opened.

'Come on, boy. It can't take that long to buy a stamp.'

'Sorry. Just coming.' Henry went out again. A short silence followed wherein Graham leaned forward from his book of stamps with a suspicious look on his face.

'Oh. So your uncle does know that you're posting a letter,' he whispered, tearing out a single stamp. I handed over the money but he held on to the stamp. Glancing round at the clock he said 'The collection is due any minute. I tell you what. Why don't you give me the letter and I'll make sure that it goes off?'

'Yes. That's fine.' Why is he whispering? Or am I going deaf? I handed over the letter. Graham grabbed it eagerly and smiled.

'We'll see you again soon, I hope. Take care of yourself. And don't worry.' He winked in a most theatrical fashion and I left the shop convinced that Henry had good cause to shun this village of unpredictable lunatics. I mean, what on earth could that have been about? In due course I was to find out.

eighteen

In which manacles are forged in the shed

This latest episode in the shop left me appreciating one of the few aspects of Henry's character that could be called a quality. In fact, his behaviour compared quite favourably with that of the villagers and their minister. I had gone to the shop expecting the cold treatment of my last visit but had instead been greeted like a long lost son – and, if anything, I found this excessive friendliness even more alarming. It was in this area that Henry compared rather well. Whatever else could be said about him, and there was plenty, no one could call Henry unpredictable. Whatever the time or place you knew that you could always rely on Henry. To be an absolute bastard. What's more, and perhaps also to his credit, this reliability was the result of his honesty. Henry said what he thought. It just so happened that what he thought was utterly unspeakable, but then you can't have everything.

By now I was extremely suspicious of the folk of the village. They seemed prone to changing like the mountain weather. All was sweetness and light until I said the wrong thing. But now the charm had returned once more and I was sure that there had to be some ulterior motive. Well, whatever it was it could jolly well remain a motive and not turn into an action. From now on I would avoid the village like the plague.

This personal vow meant that yet another part of the glen was now out of bounds, along with the forbidden hills. There was little left apart from the loch which I now felt to be uncomfortably close to the village. My choice of possible stamping grounds was being steadily narrowed down to the confines of the house. And, of course, the garden.

I was to have the garden to myself the following day. It was another of those mornings when I was allowed to wake up naturally, rather than being shaken out of bed by the dawn refrain of the hot and cold. When I noticed this strange silence I was almost prepared to take a gamble on Henry having disappeared again and stay where I was, in bed. But I thought it better to be safe than sorry and arrived in the kitchen on the stroke of eight. I needn't have worried. There on the table was a note virtually identical to that of last week. Henry would be away for most of the day and I should feed myself. There seemed little point in going out and about, not when there was no Henry to avoid, so I chose to spend the day in the quiet of the garden, reading and sunbathing.

Perhaps I overdid the sunbathing. I was quite sure that I had baked my brain. In fact, there was a definite smell of burning which I was sure emanated from the inside of my head. I spent the latter part of the afternoon lying down in the shade of my room, wondering if it would help if I poured water in my ear. After an hour or so my frontal lobes stopped sizzling and I sat myself at the desk, staring dreamily out of the window. It was then that I saw Henry coming up the hill. He was moving at a much slower pace than his usual quick march and, as I watched him, for the first time I wondered where he might have been.

He obviously wasn't going to provide an answer, his usual supper silence being accompanied by a slight sense of melancholy, the same abstracted air that had hung about him the week before when he had returned from a similar mystery expedition. We parted as soon as we had eaten, Henry saying nothing but a quiet 'Goodnight' before vanishing into his study.

The following morning he seemed to have recovered, and he

cursed Oscar in the kitchen in his usual eloquent manner. At the breakfast table he spoke without looking up.

'And what did you get up to yesterday, boy?'

'Nothing much. I just read in the garden.'

He looked over. 'No more little jaunts up the mountains, then?'

I looked down, embarrassed more by my daft motives on that day of escape than by the resulting predicament.

'No. Not at all. I stayed here all the time.'

'Good. Because I would not be at all pleased otherwise.'

'I know. That's why I stayed in the garden.' Henry nodded and it was not until we had finished eating that he spoke again.

'Still, a garden, even the size of mine, soon becomes a small place for a child. It would easy to grow bored and restless, in which case you might be tempted to wander again. Mightn't you?'

I said nothing, but sat trying to look as if the thought had never crossed my mind. Henry continued. 'Hmm. Yes, you might wander again, and didn't I say after your last little adventure that we would have to do something about that? Yes. I believe I did.' He stood up, cleared the table and was in the study before I could even think of asking what he had in mind.

It was to be a tense day. I thought of going into the garden but felt safer in my room. I watched Henry walk across the garden, past the vegetables and into the shed, from which I had occasionally seen him emerge with gardening tools. This time Henry did not emerge immediately and my curiosity was aroused. A faint creaking sound was followed by a loud thud, then silence reigned once more until the next loud bang, at which the chickens began to propel themselves around the enclosure like the Keystone Kops. It was when the clanging started that I began to worry. I turned over in my mind visions of the chain which would curtail my wanderings. Just how far from the tree in the garden would it allow me to roam? There was another thud, a squeak or two and then some more bangings which seemed to bring the work to some kind of end, for Henry soon appeared, wiping his hands on a rag, and crossed back over to the house. Within a few minutes he had returned to the shed, carrying a sinister wooden box which I could not see very clearly. The next ten minutes in the shed were quiet. Too quiet.

This time when Henry came back into the house he stayed there, his dreadful task obviously completed.

My fearful curiosity was further heightened by the silence, of lunch. I sat through the entire meal waiting for Henry to say 'I have just been . . . ' followed by an explanation of what he had been up to. But there was no hint at all of whatever had been going on in the shed.

After lunch Henry seemed to be safely ensconced in his study, so I decided to risk a trip into the garden. I planted myself in the usual corner with a book, pencils and paper. I wasn't in the mood for reading, my mind being far too agitated by the thing in the shed, so I decided instead to indulge my creative side with a little light drawing. I attempted to capture one of the trees in the garden, but found it a bit too complicated, realising after the first three dozen leaves that this would never work. I had always been better at buildings. They tended to oblige with nice straight lines and sensible proportions. However, the main reason that I sat in this corner was that it was out of sight of the house, and I didn't really fancy moving out into the open, so that rather cut down the choice of sketchable buildings. Apart, that is, from the shed. The Shed. It was within my line of sight, if I moved round this bush a little.

I remembered being told at school to try and get a feel for the general shape of the subject, rather than just plunge straight in with excruciating detail. Like leaves. So, I started with a sketched outline, lots of those hairy little lines that artists use. The line of the roof, the walls, a line for the ground, and then fill in the details. The felt roof was easy enough, grey speckles mostly, with a few broad nail heads. Now the planks that cross the side. One, then two, then that one that stops on either side of the window. The Window. That shed has a window in it. And windows are notorious for their transparency. So I might just be able to see whatever is in there . . . I'm sure that it's probably nothing at all. Henry wouldn't really go so far as to . . . Or would he? Only one way to find out.

I laid my paper aside and, checking that I wasn't being watched, began to stroll innocently across the lawn as if to have a look at the chickens as they strutted mechanically around their yard. When I got to the wire I stopped, checked once more that it was safe, and shuffled sideways to the shed. The window had obviously been designed with the exclusion of nosy little boys in mind. Even on arch-racking tiptoe it was too high for me to see in. I was about to give in when I spotted the bucket over by the bean row. It was an old tin bucket that Henry used for weeding. I was delighted to find it empty, pressed to see if it was stout enough to support me, then stalked back over to the shed. I was just approaching the window when Pavlov's chickens caught sight of their bell of a bucket and the most awful racket ensued. I tried to show them that it was empty but they remained unconvinced and merely squawked all the louder. As they clustered ravenously at the wire I began to panic and decided to make one rushed attempt at my espionage. I upturned the bucket on the ground and was about to step up to the window when a voice boomed above the squawking.

'What are you doing to my chickens, boy?'

I stood like Eros on one leg atop the bucket, leaping down with a speed which I hoped might exceed that of light and thus render my indiscretion invisible.

'What are you doing?'

What can one be doing by a mysterious shed window with an upturned bucket? There seemed few alternatives, but I had to think of one pretty fast. Henry strode up to me as, in a moment of pathetic inspiration, I began to size up the bucket with my pencil in true artistic fashion. A little addition to the composition? Maybe not. Henry looked once at the bucket, once at the chickens, twice at the shed and then gave me a long stare while he put two and two together.

'Aha! As with the Roman geese, the barbarian is revealed in his stealthy ambitions. And just what are you doing?'

There seemed no choice other than to um and er, so I did.

'I um . . . er . . .'

'I see. Trying to find out what I have in my shed, eh?' Well just remember the adverse effects of curiosity on feline well-being.'

'Oh? Yes. Well, I um . . . er . . . '

'And also remember that patience is a virtue. You will find out what I have been doing in the shed. All in good time.'

Henry then smiled in a way that told me that even my worst fears would pale into insignificance when faced by the reality of Whatever was in the Shed . . .

nineteen

❧

The Thing in the Shed

I spent a sleepless night with my almost constant companion rampant paranoia. Every time I had been sobered out of one absurd fantasy, be it Henry's murderous tendencies or his violent revenge, it only took a few days before I had managed to summon up some other spectre with which to petrify myself. Today's contender was the Thing in the Shed and I was reminded of the sinister clangings and thuds by the boiler, which woke me in good time for breakfast.

The meal itself passed in virtual silence, nothing being said – although while preparing the meal and clearing the table Henry could be heard humming quietly, and wore an expression which indicated that he was feeling very pleased with himself. I knew that this could not bode well.

After breakfast I retired to my room where I waited with a growing sense of black anticipation. Henry was in the study and I kept a constant watch out of the window. An hour passed. I was just changing position during my vigil, to relieve the pins and needles, when, to my horror, I saw Henry crossing the lawn and heading straight for the shed. He vanished inside and the hairs on the back of my neck stood to attention as the squeakings began again. Two sharp clangs and then silence. Henry reappeared and strolled across the lawn. He was a long way below, but I could tell by the way that his beard moved that he was laughing.

I waited. Nothing happened. I waited some more. Finally, I heard it. The sound of footsteps on the stairs. They stopped and I heard the toilet door close. I sighed with relief, but I had relaxed too soon. The door was unbolted below and the feet continued up the stairs. No doubt along with the rest of Henry. Three, two, one and . . . The opening of the door wasn't really as dramatic as it had been billed, and Henry stooped into the room.

'Ah, there you are, boy.' There I certainly was. 'I wonder if you would be so good as to come with me. I have something that I would like you to try for size.' He smiled again and I knew that this was it.

Down the stairs I followed him, through the kitchen, out of the lobby and inexorably across the lawn. We halted by the shed.

'Wait here, boy.' Henry opened the door and stepped inside. There was a scuffling sound, then the door was kicked open as Henry backed out.

'There,' he said 'It was your father's. The handlebars were cooperative enough, but I had the devil's own job trying to lower the saddle. Had to leave it in oil over night. Well, don't just stand there, try it for size.'

Utterly astonished I stepped forward and carefully swung my leg over the saddle of the old black bicycle with the wicker basket.

'Yes, that should do,' said Henry. 'Besides, it won't go down any lower. Now you shall be able to wander and explore without having to resort to the near fatal heights.'

I was in a state of shock, but managed to mutter 'Thank you. Very much. I er . . . '

'Just remember meal-times – and not after dark, as you have no lights. This part of the world is not overly plagued by traffic of any kind but exercise due caution all the same.'

'Yes. Of course, I . . . '

'This should be a suitable way of keeping you out of my hair without the risks which could lead to further inconvenience.' With that he turned abruptly and strode back to the house, pausing only briefly at the door to call 'If you see anyone I know, run them over.'

I was left perched on the saddle, feet only just touching the ground, and quietly turning an interesting shade of pink. Yet again, in the comfort and privacy of my own mind I had managed to summon up spectres who did nothing more than make a complete fool of me. Or rather, I made a complete fool of myself, and sometimes it is even worse to be privately humiliated, as it doesn't even allow the relative comfort of fighting back against your tormentors. And it is doubly worse when it is not the first time that such private embarrassment has resulted from an excessively active imagination. This time not only had my fears been as absurd and unfounded as usual, but the truth behind this latest self-induced nightmare had turned out to be positively wonderful. The problem of the ever-diminishing number of possible destinations had been removed in one fell swoop. This ancient and noble machine meant freedom, freedom from the house and Henry and freedom from the confines of this one small glen with its deranged inhabitants. This fine black steed, with its (now permissible) links with my father was simultaneously able to provide a much-needed connection to my past and a bridge to an exciting future when I would roam the length and breadth of the Highlands. With this trusty mount (I had joined the cavalry now after years as a foot soldier) I could conquer the world.

Unfortunately I had not reckoned with conquering the hill out of the glen. From the house it was plain sailing, leaving the gravel of the drive to hear the tyres hum on the tarmac of the road as I gathered pace down the hill, up and down on the bridge (rearranging several vertebrae in the process), then rushing around the corner and onto the road to the world. Sadly, momentum is not what it used to be. A pitiful twenty or so yards were all that I managed before being forced to change to lowest gear and battle laboriously up the hill. Perhaps another hundred yards had been wound past by the pedals before I saw enough sense to get off and walk. It was a long haul, but not as long as the other side whose endless downhill greeted me as I finally crested the hill. These great slopes in and out of the glen were a small price to pay in order to be allowed to enter the world at large. I was to spend the rest of that week in an orgy of exploration which stretched from breakfast to supper, and which was blessed by the most glorious weather. I returned to the house at the end of each day with a slightly browner face than before and a pleasant aching tiredness in my pedalling legs.

After the daily effort of the glen road I was wise enough to avoid any of the particularly hilly areas which the map would admit to. Instead I concentrated on the valley round the river Spey, which undulated only gently and provided a thousand opportunities for side-tracks. I saw the river alive with leaping salmon and the great mythical mass of the Cairngorms rising in the distance, their northern slopes still bleached by snow even in the height of summer. Further still I watched the ospreys of Loch Garten who were, this year, almost entirely undisturbed by visitors. Those who knew the area well would have been surprised by this strange absence of tourists and travellers, but to me it was a blessing. The roads were empty, the sun was shining, only the gentlest of breezes disturbed the roadside grass and Henry was so many miles away.

Even at times when he was less than miles away, on the other side of the table, Henry had become just a little more tolerable. He was no doubt as pleased to have found a way to maintain his solitude as I was to get away from him and, when we did meet up, the atmosphere was not as cold and unpleasant as it had been. Henry would sometimes even ask where I had been and, in my excitement, I would forget myself and describe, in one hurried jumble, the day that had passed. Henry would nod politely and occasionally add further information about the places and things that I described and I would leave the table feeling as if we had almost had a conversation.

These little exchanges were only marred once when Henry, replying to my observation that there were very few people about, remarked that 'Most animals go home to die.' This served as a reminder that this was still Henry and that time was still short.

twenty

Just when I was running out of mysteries . . .

Sleepless nights were impossible after my endless days of pedalling and I was up in the mornings before the larks could get a song in edgeways. I sometimes even managed to be up before the boiler could begin its latest oratorio and, with Henry's permission, would prepare breakfast and a parcel of sandwiches before he had even finished his bath.

In fact, so adept had I grown at wakening before Henry that when I surfaced one morning to the sound of silence I immediately assumed that it still must be before the bathing hour. I unfolded the bedside map and began to plan the day's itinerary. Once that had been decided I ventured out from beneath the covers for a weather check. It was then that, as I was prone to doing, I received something of a surprise.

I had not, my watch kindly informed me, risen before Henry: I had in fact wakened to one of those days. One of the days on which Henry disappeared. This in a way was a blessing. Now that I had solved the various mysteries of Father and Henry, the Thing in the Shed and so on, life was lacking a little in neurotic excitement. I needed another dark puzzle with which to enliven my uncharacteristically happy brain, and here it was on a plate. The Disappearances of Henry. It was quarter past seven. I had never been up this early on a disappearing day and assumed that Henry must already have gone. However, whilst performing a passable imitation of washing at the sink I heard, amidst the splashings, the sound of feet on the gravel outside. At first this caused one of my frequent bouts of panic. Perhaps they, the villagers, also knew about Henry's regular vanishing act. They knew that I was all alone. They were coming to get me. Still dripping, I crept to the window. To a mixture of relief and disappointment I saw that the army of torch-bearing scythe-wielding peasants was in fact just Henry leaving the drive. I was about to go back to my ablutions when I spotted it, there in Henry's hand as he walked along by the hedge. The bold burst of colour standing out from the sombre brown of his tweeds could only be one thing. Henry was carrying a bunch of flowers!

I could barely believe what I had seen. Henry with a bunch of flowers. There could be only one explanation. Henry must have an admirer, or vice versa, whom he visits once a week, creeping out first thing in the morning to avoid detection.

I spent the rest of that morning, and most of the day, only half concentrating on my cycling, the vision of the flower-bearing Henry more powerful in my imagination than anything I happened to see on my travels. There were only one or two niggling little details to be cleared up before I could settle on an explanation, but it wasn't like me to let evidence interfere with my conclusions. If Henry was courting, then why was that the one day on which he didn't have a bath? And why did he come home looking so subdued and sad? Drawing on my full ten years' experience of the ways of the world I was soon able to account for these minor problems. The bath business was probably some old Highland custom

Bathe not in the morn
Lest love be torn . . .

or something like that. As for the sadness of Henry at the end of the day, well, the pre-pubescent pushbike Freud had it all worked out. It was quite plain that poor old Henry's affections were being

113

spurned. Unrequited love was tormenting his delicate soul, causing him to vent his frustration and wrath on the world at large and me and Oscar in particular. Still, who could blame him now that the tragic truth was out? Certainly not me. I vowed to be more understanding of poor Henry from now on. I had stumbled upon his sad secret and could not be so heartless as to blame him for the pain that it caused.

My head was so awash with virtuous and forgiving thoughts that I ran straight into the grass verge and very nearly came to grief on the crossbar, but I recovered enough to plan my return to Halfway House, which I now saw in a totally different light. The angel of mercy pedalled his way home.

I arrived back in plenty of time for supper, parked the bike in the shed, which no longer held any great secrets, and made my way indoors. I sat for a while in my room, trying to decide on the best way of approaching this delicate subject, and the best way to comfort Henry and give him hope. Somewhat uninspired, I decided to play it by ear and slowly descended the stairs armed with new insight and a mission.

Henry was just serving up supper when I arrived and we sat down together. Silence reigned once more at the table and, yes, Henry did have that sad air about him. I watched his face carefully as he ate. After a while he became aware of my gaze and looked up. I smiled what I took to be my most benign and understanding smile, a 'don't worry old chap I know how you feel' sort of a smile. Henry glared back quizzically, so I further exaggerated my saintly facial contortion, just in case he hadn't picked it up the first time. At this Henry raised one eyebrow, shook his head and sighed loudly before returning to his meal. A sigh. The poignancy of the moment was almost unbearable, and yet my silent communication seemed to be falling on deaf eyes. I decided to risk a light conversational gambit.

'Nice day, wasn't it?'

'Hmm,' Henry grunted and carried on eating. It was clear that he was a bit shy about the whole thing and would need a bit of coaxing, a few subtle hints to get the conversation going.

'It was a good day for going out, wasn't it?'

Henry looked up. 'Quite,' he said, and looked down again.

'I had a really good day.' There was a so-what silence. 'Did you?' I continued.

'No.' That was all he would part with.

We ate some more. The silence continued. It was obvious that Henry didn't realise how much I knew and I was running out of time – the meal would soon be over. I had to keep trying.

'Not such a good day then?'

'NO!' It was loud, rather frightening and meant to bring an end to the conversation, but I was too thick-skinned and -skulled to be deterred. The matter must be addressed more directly. I waited for an appropriate moment.

'Still no luck then?' I smiled sympathetically. Henry drew his cutlery together with a clatter.

'I have absolutely no idea, boy, what on earth you are talking about. Nor do you I suspect, but I get the distinct impression that, should you ever grow older, you will be the kind of person who makes rail journeys intolerable.'

'I'm sorry. I was just wondering if . . .'

'Whatever you were wondering, if it concerns me, is none of your business. Kindly remember that and goodnight.'

I could take a hint. I skulked off upstairs without a word. Gone was the Henry of the last few days with his polite snippets of conversation. This was a Henry back to old form once more, if not worse. I even entertained, for a moment, the thought that I might just be wrong, perhaps it was something other than unrequited love that made Henry the way he was. That would be a shame, after I had worked out so carefully why Henry had changed from the charming man that my father had known – it had all fitted into place. Perhaps he was just a bit too sensitive about it at the moment, given time he might confess. But my wait to hear the truth of the matter was to be interrupted by the dramatic events of the following twenty-four hours.

twenty-one

*In which there is a spot
of bad weather*

Meanwhile, a great storm was brewing. No, not that storm, not the great metaphorical one, just an ordinary common or garden Scottish summer typhoon. Dense grey clouds were sent scudding up the glen to break like waves on the hill tops. Trees began to hiss and cower as the wind tugged at their leaves and sent patterns of wild energy weaving across the mountainside bracken.

The whole house seemed to shudder as the gale rose, howling round the corners, rattling the window frames, pushing and pulling at curtains until the draughty gap was pulled shut against the horizontal sheets of rain which splashed across my desk, leaving damp blisters on the pages of my drawing pad. I switched on the light before closing the curtains against the prematurely dark sky then dropped myself into the corner armchair. It was all a bit of a disappointment. Henry had either failed to appreciate my solicitous enquiries or else he was just too touchy about it. Perhaps it would be better to wait until another day when Henry, and the elements, were in a better mood. Unable to think of anything better to do I opted for reading in bed for a while as the house creaked and sighed around me like a storm wracked galleon. Even lashed to my bunk, and with one of my trustiest men at the helm, it was some time

116

before I finally grew accustomed to the banshee wind and waves of hammering rain, and it was midnight before I finally drifted off to sleep.

In the morning the birds sounded the all clear, the wind had exhausted itself and the sun had returned from a less blustery side of the world. However, the abatement of the gale was not the only silence I could hear. For the second morning in a row the boiler was silent. And there were footsteps on the gravel outside. From the window I could see Henry, without flowers, staring back up at me. I smiled nervously but he seemed not to have noticed and strode off in an agitated manner round to the back of the house. He was even late for breakfast, which was most unlike him, and still appeared to be in a far from good mood. He did, however, speak without any prompting on my part.

'I am faced by something of a dilemma, boy.'

This was it. He was about to pour his heart out.

'The question is,' he continued, 'is it worth the effort to repair one's ravaged roof when the world may end at any minute, doing unimaginable damage to the tiles and guttering?' He sighed, wearily depositing the toast and himself at the table. 'Sleep well last night?' he asked.

'Well, it was a bit noisy.'

'Quite. I've just been doing a small inspection tour. Most of the slates seem to have stayed fairly firmly in place. And at least the chimneys have not deposited parts of themselves in the garden. However, a sizeable portion of the guttering has detached itself from the front of the house.'

'Oh,' I said, my disappointment at the mundane nature of this dilemma sounding unintentionally sympathetic.

'Tempting though it may be to postpone one's house repairs until Armageddon polishes off the job, there is a rather more pressing problem. One of the pines beyond the garden wall has suffered a fair bit of damage. The next reasonably strong wind will, I fear, send it toppling onto the chickens. Hideously ugly though they may be, they do have their uses. Besides, the toolshed is also in danger. And with it your bicycle,' he added dramatically.

'Oh!' It was suddenly far less mundane.

'Good. Now that I have your interest in the problems, I wonder if you might be good enough to assist me in my efforts to repair the damage?'

'Yes. Certainly,' I replied. Not that I would have said no, but the bicycle had to be saved. And Henry's omelettes definitely justified the rescue of the chickens. Besides, I was a little flattered to be asked to help. It made me feel important.

We finished breakfast and Henry said that he was going off to change. I waited in the kitchen until he returned wearing a set of well-seasoned blue overalls, liberally adorned with paint and muck.

'Might as well look the part,' he remarked. 'Besides, Harris tweed suits are not ideal apparel for repairing roofs. Unless, of course, one is planning a fatal fall, in which case it may be appropriate to be smartly dressed for the wake. Now then, this is the plan. Firstly, you shall assist me in carrying the ladders round to the front of the house. Then I shall climb up the front while you make your way upstairs. You may then support the renegade guttering while I re-attach it. Got that?'

I felt as if I should salute or snap my heels together, but made do with an enthusiastic nod. The ladders were duly carried from the shed and I left Henry to clatter them up the front of the house while I ran upstairs to my room and opened the window. Henry set the base of the ladder firmly, then climbed up until his head was level with mine, but a few feet to the left. From one pocket of his overall he produced a length of coarse string, which he proceeded to tie around the drooping gutter, whose bracket had been torn from the wood of the eves.

'Right, boy. When I throw the string you catch hold of it and pull.' He tossed an end towards me. The second attempt was more successful and I reeled it in, taking the strain as Henry lifted the half-pipe up into place.

'Now then, just hold that in place while I fix it back on.' I held on tight as Henry adjusted the bracket and proceeded to screw it into a fresh piece of wood. The operation was fairly straightforward and we had it finished in a matter of ten minutes.

'All right, boy, you can let it go now.' Henry perched at the top of the ladder, checking his handiwork before carefully unknotting the string. 'Right, that should do. Meet me downstairs so we can sort out phase two, then you'll be free to go off and do whatever you want to do.'

Back in the garden the ladder was exchanged in the shed for a formidable-looking axe which, just for a change, I did not assume to be intended for some fiendish purpose. There was no way to get to the tree beyond the back wall except by walking to the front of the house and then round the outside of the garden. When we reached the tree Henry rolled up his sleeves and squinted up into the sun at the precarious balancing act going on between the upper and lower storeys of the trunk.

'I can't see any other way round this problem. It will have to be the axe. Pity really, it's not a bad specimen, but needs must. Now, boy, if you stand out of the way on the other side I shall endeavour to make a sufficiently large cut so that we can fell it away from the garden.'

Beyond the wall the chickens muttered and clucked, unaware that at any minute the sky might fall on their heads. Henry took a deep breath and swung the axe back. It came round in a wide arc and bit hard into the wood. He brought it round again, this time cutting from below, working towards removing a wedge.

'Haven't done this for years,' he called out between whacks. 'Either the trees are getting tougher or I'm getting older.' He kept swinging, but called out again.

'By the way, boy' – there was a whack – 'I meant to say' – grunt whack – 'something of an apology' – whack – 'for yesterday' He gave it one more swing then stopped temporarily. He was sweating profusely and had turned rather pink.

'It's not that I regret being objectionable, after all, it is something of a vocation for me. No, it's more a matter of motive. Calm and honest statement of the unpleasant truths about people is one thing' – he began to swing again – 'but yesterday I fear I spoke out of mere petty bad temper.' The blows were slowing and Henry was beginning to show the strain, either of the chopping or of the apology. 'And that is another matter altogether. It is not one of the days on which I am particularly approachable.'

What is?

'So I'm afraid that I must apologise.'

He resumed his assault on the tree. It was proving a lot hardier than it looked. Surprised by Henry's unusually pleasant demeanour, and a little worried by his reddening face, I offered to take a turn.

'No, don't be silly, boy. This won't take long.' He took another few swings, muttering as he did 'I hope those wretched birds appreciate what I'm . . .' His words tailed off as the axe skidded off the wood and seemed to pull him along with it. Henry struggled to regain his balance, staggering a little, then stood very still, breathing heavily.

'I seem to . . .' His face crumpled in pain, followed shortly by his legs. I ran over, terrified, to where he lay, folded awkwardly in the bracken.

'Henry. Henry?' I cried.

He half opened his eyes, in obvious pain. His breathing was a struggle and his voice a croak.

'Don't just stand there, boy . . .'

'What then?' I had very little experience of the health problems suffered by elderly misanthropic lumberjacks.

'Get some help. MacIntyre, in the village . . .'

'The doctor?'

'No, the plumber. Who do you think?'

'Right. Of course. Is there a phone or something?'

'No, you'll have to use the bicycle.'

'Shall I help you indoors or . . . is there anything I mean . . .?'

'No. Stop gibbering and go. And hurry up about it.'

Henry lay back amongst the bracken, breathing quickly and cursing.

I barely even knew what I was doing as I launched myself off round the wall and into the garden. I hauled the bike from the shed, getting into a terrible tangle of pedals and doors before bouncing down onto the grass. I mounted up there and then on the lawn, skidded over the gravel and sped, already breathless, down the hill. I was soon moving with such velocity that even the most frantic pedalling failed to engage the wheels so I free-wheeled impatiently as the wind stole what was left of my breath and a bee recklessly collided with my forehead. Abandoning my stomach on the bridge I pedalled furiously with the hill's momentum along the manse road.

I had neither the time nor the inclination to slow down when the Reverend Murchie stepped out of his gate and into the road. He sprang back like a broken jack in the box, grabbed for support on the still open gate then receded, with a flailing of arms, into a flower-bed. I glanced back briefly, feeling that, even if I was too late, my trip had not been entirely in vain.

Round into the High Street I rode, halting too fast for my own good in front of the first, rather alarmed, person that I saw.

'The doctor. Where is he?'

'Doctor MacIntyre is it you're after?'

'Yes!' I almost yelled.

'Up round the corner there. Last house on the left.'

'Thanks,' I called back as I panted off up the hill and round the corner towards where a vaguely familiar Land Rover was parked. I dropped the bike with a clatter, wheel still spinning, and ran up to the door. I held the bell down for as long as even my panic would allow as polite. I waited, and was about to ring again when the door opened.

'All right, all right, where's the fire?' said the portly man with the napkin in his hand.

'No. Not a fire. I want the doctor. Is he here?'

'Yes, that's me.'

'Well, you've got to come quickly. It's my uncle. He's collapsed and . . .'

'Your uncle? And who might that be?'

'Henry. Henry Dundas.'

'Henry? Ill? That's not like him. It's against his principles . . .'

'But he's collapsed.'

'Hmm. And in the middle of my bloody breakfast. Typical. Well just hang on for a moment and I'll be with you as soon as I can.'

He disappeared into the house, emerging a few moments later with a black medical bag.

'Is he up at the house?'

'Yes.'

'Right. Chuck your bike in the back and we'll get going.'

The engine started noisily and we shot off down the High Street.

'Henry ill? Now there's a turn up for the books.' We turned the corner. 'And you say he's your uncle?'

'Well, some sort of great uncle. On my father's side.'

'Ah. So you must be Sam's wee boy.'

'That's right.'

'Well well. I'm Doctor MacIntyre. Very pleased to meet you. I knew your Dad very well when he was a lad.'

Up ahead, by the kirk, the Reverend was walking along the roadside. He turned to scowl at the oncoming vehicle, then saw who was sitting in it. He looked very angry and made as if to flag us down, shouting something about young hooligans. I grew rather alarmed as the doctor slowed a little and began to wind down his window. However, as we passed the minister all he did was lean out of the window and shout 'Och. Up your bum, Murchie!' then roared off over the bridge. It seemed that Henry was not the only one around here who abused men of the cloth.

'One thing I have in common with your uncle. Cannot abide the little bugger.'

The multitude of gears soon had us up the hill and in no time we had stopped in the drive.

'Where is he then?'

'Round there. At the back of the wall.'

The doctor followed me round to the half-chopped tree. There was a Henry-shaped patch of flattened bracken, but the man himself had disappeared.

'Well,' said the doctor, 'either he's moved or he's died and decomposed pretty damn quickly.'

We retraced our steps round into the garden and finally found Henry sitting in the kitchen. He was still very red and his breathing had slowed only slightly. Dr MacIntyre pulled up a chair beside him.

'Now then, Henry, what ails you?'

'It is a measure of just how desperate I must be that I have actually sent for a quack like you, MacIntyre.'

'Oh ye of little faith.' Then he spoke more seriously. 'What's the trouble then?'

'I collapsed. I can't breathe. My chest feels as if it has been embraced by an enormous car-crusher. My head is swimming and I am in mortal agony.'

'But apart from that you're fine?' said the doctor producing his stethoscope. He examined Henry carefully, nodding from time to time and emitting the small 'm-hm's that doctors emit to give the impression that they know what they are doing.

'Aye,' he said at last unblocking his ears, 'it's your heart. What have you been up to now?'

'Just trying to fell a tree.'

The doctor expressed his balanced medical opinion.

'You silly old fart. It's no wonder your bloody ticker gave way. How many times have I told you? You should know better by now. And you're damn lucky it wasn't far worse.'

I stood in the background, utterly astounded that anyone should speak to Henry as if he was human. The doctor unglazed my eyes.

'A glass of water for your uncle, please. Here you are, Henry, take these and rest do you hear me. Rest! You make sure that the old fool stays flat on his bum, or even better, on his back.'

I nodded earnestly. Henry groaned. His breathing had acquired a gentler pace.

'You do realise, MacIntyre, that it took exceptional circumstances for me to call for you.'

'Oh yes. And what might those be?' he asked, closing up his bag.

'You see,' continued Henry, 'to have died within weeks, or possibly days, of the end of the world, the final cure for the terrestrial mange that is mankind, would have been too darkly ironic a joke, even for me.'

'Oh! I see. As you are personally unable to do anything about it, you at least want to be around as a spectator.'

'Precisely,' said Henry.

'You don't get any better do you?' laughed the doctor.

'Nor do you. But needs must.'

'Well, I wouldn't worry if I were you, Henry. You won't die. Nobody would have you. However, just to be on the safe side, make sure that you get that rest and try to hang on so you can peg out with the rest of us. It'll save me the bother of rushing out in the middle of my breakfast.' He stood up and made for the door, turning as he left.

'And just remember, Henry, no more felling trees. You're supposed to be inhuman, not superhuman.' He disappeared with a roar of laughter.

'And there was me thinking that sarcasm was the lowest form of wit,' muttered Henry. He sat very still for a while then rose slowly and began to walk with great care towards the study.

'I'm going to lie down for a while. Waken me if the war starts.'

twenty-two

In which Henry is somewhat below par

By suppertime the war still hadn't started. Nor had Henry appeared. He was still shut away in the study, from which no sound emerged. It wasn't like him to be late for a mealtime. Despite the doctor's jolly tone it had been quite clear that something was seriously wrong. Henry was having trouble with his heart, as Father had done, and that was serious. He may have had many faults, and I had been made to feel less than welcome at Halfway House, but, just recently, Henry had grown a little more tolerant and tolerable. Besides which, the fact that he was capable of being ill and of being spoken to by at least one person in a spirit of coarse badinage seemed to suggest that he might be human after all. It seemed a long shot, but, with this evidence, plus the affair and my conclusion that he had changed over the years, it seemed worth the gamble. Yes, I would be nice to Henry. But this time with a little more caution and a careful avoidance of possibly sensitive areas.

I sat down at the table, wondering how best to begin my campaign. Oscar sat in the corner looking bored. Henry still hadn't appeared and it was well past the supper hour. I was beginning to feel rather worried. Even worse, I was beginning to feel hungry. It was the gentle rumbling of my stomach which first suggested the plan. I must

125

take care of Henry in his hour of need. This would not only repay him for the attention lavished upon me in my sick-bed, but would also help to guarantee his continued existence.

Keeping Henry alive was, I realised, a necessary evil. Without him I would be forced to leave the hills and return to Aunt Margaret. After carefully considering the undesirability of such a fate, any remaining genuine charity on my part could soon be accounted for by the intense spiritual pride which invariably accompanied all my finer thoughts and deeds. Still, whatever the motives, there were certain practicalities to be overcome before my philanthropic plans could reach fruition. The first step in caring for an ailing Henry would be to feed him. Now, I could knock together a cheese sandwich with the best of them, but was that really ideal invalid fodder? Besides, the very sight of my hacked and mutilated bread slices might be enough to cause a relapse. No, that wouldn't do. Invalids must be fed with broth. It was traditional. Thus began a search through the myriad cupboards for a tin of soup. Within five minutes the kitchen looked like a well-used advent calendar, but still no soup had been found. There remained no alternative, it would have to be done from scratch.

One thing the search had uncovered was an epic blue tome on cookery and household management, packed to the gunwales with information on how to prepare a nine-course meal for four on a budget of 2/6, with enough left over for a stout set of stays. This book was far more cooperative than its ornithological colleague had been, and revealed soups in the index just where they ought to be. I browsed through the appropriate section, skipping swiftly over those concoctions consisting of bits of animals that I wouldn't even have the stomach to throw away. A few flicks backwards and forwards eventually left me settled on carrot and lentil. It seemed to be the simplest of the bunch and was one for which I knew all the contents were available.

Well, here goes nothing. Miraculously still equipped with the requisite number of fingers, I tipped the chopped onions and carrots into a pan of hot oil (some of which had to be poured down the sink lest the vegetables be French fried). There was an almighty hiss, which chased Oscar from his corner, and made me duck as hot oil spat vindictively at my face. I hauled the pan off the gas and turned it down as far as it would go, i.e. out. Relighting the stove I stirred the vegetables until brown. Carrots? Brown? Oh, until onions are brown. Carrots must be soft. There are a lot of carrots in there . . . Never mind, what's next? Add lentils. Try to retrieve mountain of lentils deposited by collapsing bag. Burn hand. Swear quietly then give up. Fill pan with water, bring to boil, simmer until cooked, then season to taste. It was all a bit too easy really, too 'straight-from-the-book', what it needed was the personal touch, the hacking up of a small potato or two then bunging them in as well. The whole mixture was brought to the boil, salted and peppered with caution, then left to simmer.

After spending a happy twenty minutes engrossed in the cakes and biscuits I was pleasantly astonished to discover that my concoction, which had received a handful of mixed herbs as a parting shot, was in fact edible, and even bore more than a passing resemblance to soup. In my usual inimitable fashion I sliced some bread then prepared a tray with salt, pepper, cup of tea, bread and butter, and a bowl of my soup.

Nervously I knocked on the study door. There was no response. This made me even more nervous, so I knocked again, loudly. This time there was a startled grunt and Henry called sleepily –

'What is it?'

'It's me.'

'Yes, I thought it might be.'

'I've brought you something.'

'All right, come in then.'

I turned the handle, admitted at last to the secret lair, as mysterious as the tomb of some pharoah, of whom Henry was performing an interesting imitation, stretched out on the settee with his arms folded across his chest. He pushed himself upright and, stretching his face in a yawn, reached for his watch.

'Good lord, is that the time? You should have wakened me.'

'But I just did.'

'Yes, I know that, but before supper . . .'

I proferred the tray.

'What's this?'

'Soup. I made it.'

'That was uncharacteristically adept of you.'

'Well, I thought that you might not be feeling too . . .'

'No, I'm not. Bring it here, boy.'

I approached the settee and carefully handed the tray to Henry, who balanced it on his lap. I hovered nearby as he picked up the spoon, staring suspiciously at the bowl in front of him. He sipped cautiously.

'Hmm. Verging on the palatable. Well, aren't you having any?'

'Yes, I thought I would . . .'

'Fetch a bowl and join me.'

'Yes. Right away.'

'And bring the pot while you're at it. I'm hungry.'

I had soon returned from the kitchen with my hands full. Henry pointed to an armchair near the head of the settee, separated from him by a small table, on which the pot was laid. Henry emptied his bowl and helped himself to some more while I sat sipping nervously, quite overawed at being invited into this inner sanctum, this book-lined den in which Henry spent so much secret time. Henry was half way through his third bowl when he spoke again.

'So much for heredity.'

'Sorry.'

'I mean, like father like son. Doesn't always apply.'

'Oh?'

'When your father was a boy I tried to make him do his share in the kitchen, tried to instruct him in the culinary arts. It was like trying to teach a tone deaf man to sing. He hadn't a clue. Mind you, in a way you had to admire him. It does take a singular talent to do what he did to food. The simplest dish, with the freshest, most wholesome ingredients, could be almost magically transformed into the most execrable mess you could possibly imagine.'

For the first time, in the presence of Henry, I began to laugh.

'What's so funny, boy?'

'Oh, it's just that he never got any better.'

'Hmm. Doesn't surprise me in the least.' He paused, remembering carefully. 'You know, at one time I was sure that he did it deliberately, made such an awful mess of cooking on purpose, so he wouldn't have to do it any more. But then one day I had gone out and left him to fend for himself. I arrived back earlier than expected and there he was, eating something which I thought of spreading in the garden to keep the birds off the fruit.'

I continued to giggle. It was now clear from where Father had derived his enthusiasm for cooking. It was unfortunate that he had not inherited any of Henry's innate ability. I sat quietly for a while. This seemed to be as good a time as any to probe for some more information.

'Did he come here a lot, my father?'

'Yes, I could never get rid of the wretched child. In fact, some of his books are still in your room. It all began a few years after the war when his mother was very ill. She used to send him up here from Glasgow during all his school holidays. And a few other times as well. He seemed to be here most of the time. And always getting himself into some kind of pickle.'

Henry seemed to be in a mood for reminiscence. He settled back on the settee, hands folded behind his head, staring out of the window.

'He shared with yourself a great propensity for getting wet, just so long as it didn't happen within the confines of a bath. Nearly drowned once trying to paddle across the loch on a log. One of the few things to be said in MacIntyre's favour is that he would often take him off my hands. Only time I ever got any peace, when he followed MacIntyre around on his house calls. Anyway, as I have already said, at least you don't take after him in the culinary respect. Thank you very much, that was a most enjoyable repast.'

He placed the tray on the table. I blushed in the darkening room, sure that any praise from Henry had to be honest and worth its weight in mere flattery and indulgence.

'Now then, boy, if you will excuse me, I think I will retire. I am still feeling rather tired. Thank you for your help today. Goodnight.'

We left the study together and retired to our respective rooms. I felt more relaxed and comfortable than I had ever done in Halfway House. It had been a disturbing day, a day which had unnerved Henry a little, enough to be pleasant and grateful for my help. What's more, he had thrown a little more light on the dark past

129

which had been troubling me. I was now more sure than ever that Henry must have changed over the years and might yet change back. It was now clear that Father had known him well, and had picked up quite a lot from Henry, but that now seemed quite forgivable. Perhaps Henry wasn't so bad after all. Yes, things were definitely looking up. Which usually means that they're watching something fall from above . . .

twenty-three

In which I am proved wrong. Again

I spent the following few days in or around the house. I was still a bit worried about Henry. He seemed to be much slower in his movements and generally more frail than before. I would linger near the study, checking for signs of life and occasionally being allowed to enter with a cup of tea. I would find Henry with a spread of books before him, making notes in the margins.

'Doctor MacIntyre said you should rest,' I ventured.

'So what? He doesn't know his coccyx from his humerus anyway. Besides, I am only reading, in case you hadn't noticed.'

Henry continued to abuse the poor medic, even though he hadn't hesitated in calling for him.

'I was forced to call for him that day. Couldn't bear the thought of missing all the fun.' He smiled. This was one aspect of Henry that I still could not get used to. No matter how much he seemed to have mellowed – not much really, but every little counts – his enthusiasm for the obliteration of all and sundry remained undiminished.

I had abandoned my own pro-war stance. My initial self-centred anger had matured into a gentle sadness. It was no longer the sudden intrusion of death, and the disruption that it brought, that troubled me. Instead, it was simply the absence which upset me, and I was slowly learning to come to terms with that and, the less I kicked against it, the less it tore back at me.

The more my personal grudge wore off, and the more life at Halfway House became tolerable, the less enthusiastic I became about the prospect of being fried. On the occasions when I did enter the study I was guaranteed to vanish magically as soon as Henry made any kind of move towards the wireless. The outside world, as far as I was concerned, could stay just where it was.

However, I did still deign to visit it. Once I had assured myself that Henry was likely to remain alive as long as any of us, I returned once more to my cycling explorations. It was at Henry's suggestion that I began to travel again. He complained about what he called my 'infernal fussing', solemnly swore that he would refrain from any further assaults on our arboreal neighbours and asked why didn't I go off and fall in a river somewhere. I refrained from emulating my Father's aquatic exploits and instead set off on the trusty bike, unaware that it was not planning to be quite as trusty as usual.

My first day out after Henry's funny turn was bright and blue, but with a cold ground that nibbled at the toes if left still too long. The usual route down the hill was followed, pedalling furiously over the bridge in the hope of having another crack at the minister, then round the corner for the usual desperate sprint against the inevitable loss of momentum.

From the brow of the hill you could see a long way before plunging down into the web of undulating back roads. I had not bothered with the map that morning. I was in no hurry to go anywhere in particular, a quiet drift about would suffice.

Which is precisely what I did, I drifted about. In fact, I drifted quite a distance, preoccupied by vague and inconsequential thoughts, until I found myself, at what my stomach calculated as lunchtime, in a small village divided by a burn. The sun had made more of an effort and was now beginning to turn the day into proper fly-buzzing summer. In a corner shop, a good deal less bleak than our local store, I bought an ice cream as an aperitif to my sandwiches. I sat with it on the grassy bank of the burn, just outside the shadow of a stone pack-horse bridge, beneath which minnows danced in formation in the pebble shallows. It was one of those days when nothing memorable happens, it just flows by in the heat. The kind of uneventful summer day which matures with age into a memory of something quite idyllic, where the psychotic wasp with designs on your cornet, the ant down your sock and the pins and needles-hard ground all fade from the sepia vision of childhood.

At least, this day would have qualified as idyllic until about four o'clock, when I realised that I would be cutting it a bit fine to be back in time for supper. But the only fine cutting that afternoon was performed by a fragment of glass lurking in the soft tarmac. The road became very bumpy, the bike began a rattle of complaint and I groaned a thousand groans at the sight of the roll of black flab that had once been my back tyre.

Fortunately, I had no puncture repair kit, which I had no idea how to use, so I wasted no time trying to repair the damage and just got straight down to the business of walking home. After ten minutes I resigned myself to a long plod, stopped trying to think myself back and settled down to enjoy the scenery at a brisk, but not too frantic, pace. I could see the time sail effortlessly past me, on its way home to roost in Henry's fob pocket where it would stack up the case against me. I hoped that my usefulness of the last few days would count in my favour and ignored my watch.

It was during one mild attack of worried acceleration that the horn sounded behind me. I assumed it to be an ill-mannered motorist, protesting his divine right to all available road space but, instead, the matching bulks of Dr MacIntyre and his Land Rover hove into view. He leaned out of the window.

'Having problems, lad?' I pointed ruefully at the back wheel. He shook his head solemnly.

'As a doctor I would say that your machine is suffering from an acute dose of pneumatic flaccidity. Nasty complaint. Only known cure – a lift home. Bung it in the back.'

For the second time in a few days I climbed into the high cab.

'You're a long way from home,' he said as we moved off. 'At that rate you would barely have been home by nightfall. And the worry wouldn't do Henry's heart any good would it?' He laughed. 'How's he been?'

I told him that he had been resting as far as not felling any more trees, and seemed to be on the mend.

'Good. I hope you laid down the law to him!'

'Well . . .'

'Aye. I can imagine. The old bugger can be pretty frightening if you don't know him. Mind you, he scares the wits out of everyone around here and they've known him for years.'

'Yes, he is quite difficult to get used to,' I understated.

'Aye. To say the least. Now, look at your poor dad, God rest his soul, he had a hell of a time with Henry. Spent most of his time here on that bike, or following me about on my rounds, anything to get away from his nibs. He and Henry were forced on each other. Your grannie, your dad's mum, was very ill for some time before she died. There wasn't really anywhere else for your dad to go other than Henry's. Must have been about your age when he first came here. Maybe a couple of years older. Man, he was terrified of Henry at first. Even tried to run away once . . .'

I blushed quietly but at least felt that I was not alone . . .

'He was picked up by some tourist,' the doctor continued, 'miles and miles from home. Wouldn't say where he had come from, so they called me to the police station and I was able to identify him. He regarded me as his great betrayer for a while – but we soon became great pals, once things had settled down a bit.'

'So he had a hard time with Henry too?'

'Aye, you could say that. But then, who doesn't?' He roared with laughter. 'Mind you, that's not to say that your dad didn't think a lot of Henry. Or else he wouldn't have sent you here.'

This was a reassurance that I had been looking for since I had first arrived, but at the same time it resurrected my curiosity about this particular mystery.

'So Henry hasn't got any worse then?' I asked.

'Worse? No, I wouldn't say that. Not that he hasn't tried though!'

'Then, wasn't he much nicer when my father was here?'

'Not as far as I recall.'

'But I was sure that . . .' All my carefully contrived theories were being overturned by extremely uncooperative facts.

'What makes you think that? That Henry has changed?'

'Well, I didn't think that Father would have sent me to stay with someone as horrible as Henry unless he didn't know what he was really like. Then I found out that he had even stayed with Henry.

And that some of the things that he used to say were Henry's ideas. So, I figured out that Henry must have changed since then and that was why I was sent here, because father didn't know. That he had changed.'

By some miracle of comprehension the doctor actually managed to decipher this garbled mess.

'Oh, I see,' he smiled. 'So you noticed that too.'

'Noticed what?'

'The things that the two of them said. It's very odd that. Your dad picked up quite a lot of Henry's catch-phrases. In fact, I think he picked up quite a lot from Henry in the way of ideas. Not that it seems obvious. I mean, just look at the two of them. Your dad spent so much time and worked so hard to help others, whereas Henry just sits on his backside and curses them to a man. And to their faces if he gets half a chance!' He laughed, but not quite as merrily as usual. 'Aye, it is a funny business.'

We were getting quite close to home, and beginning to climb the hill into the glen. Dr MacIntyre was very quiet, as if working something out in his head.

'You know, Henry always used to blame your dad on me. Said it was me that made him into such a "misguided do-gooding buffoon", to use his own description. Now, if that was true, if it was me that made him the way he was, I would be extremely flattered. But I don't think it's true. All right, so your dad spent a lot of time with me, on my rounds and so on, and that might have set him off on the medical trail, but as for his motives, as for whatever drove him on, I think the blame for that can be laid quite firmly at Henry's door.' He stopped and smiled. 'Not that I would say that to either of their faces. Especially not with the state of Henry's heart. The reaction it might produce would be enough to finish off at least one of us.' He laughed again, but I was impatient to hear more of this explanation. I was sure that it would clear up the puzzle. If I could understand a word of it . . .

'When I heard Henry say one of the things that my father used to say, it was then that I thought that he had picked up some of his ideas from Henry, so I was sure that Henry had changed, otherwise . . .' I tailed off, suffering from logical exhaustion.

'No, that's the funny thing about it. Your dad definitely did pick up a few ideas from Henry, but not from some previous incarnation. Henry is as constant as the stars. But not as pretty. No, Henry was just as bad then as now.'

This made no sense at all. Perhaps the doctor was as mad as the other villagers. What's more, we were nearly home . . .

'When you were wee,' said the doctor, 'and you pulled a funny face . . .' he demonstrated, 'did anyone ever say "Now you mind or the wind'll change and you'll be stuck like that"?'

I nodded.

'Well,' he continued, 'I used to think that that was what happened to your dad. Being around Henry can make you a bit nervous. Every time you start to think something nasty or mean you stop and say to yourself "Oh no, if I'm not careful I'll end up like him." And that's enough to make anyone behave . . .'

Now it was starting to make sense. Until . . .

'That's what I used to think. But I'm not so sure now.'

'But why?' I said loudly in my frustration.

He was quiet again, thinking carefully as we drove up towards the house. When he did speak, as we pulled up outside the hedge, I sensed a touch of the Henrys, that this was as much for his own benefit as mine.

'No. I'm quite sure that your dad did pick something up from Henry, rather than just react against him.' He paused. 'With my patients my attitude varies from one to the other. Some of them I like, some of them I think should be put down. All right, so you have to treat them all the same at the end of the day, but you can't help reacting to them as individuals. But look at Henry. One of his favourite boasts is that he's the only true egalitarian – he hates everyone equally, no matter who or what they are. To him all men are created equal – equally awful. Now there's the funny thing. I sometimes think that maybe, in a way, that's what your dad picked up from him . . .'

This put my back up and my jaw down.

'But, but, he didn't . . .'

'No, no. I don't mean that he hated everybody. Just that, well . . .' he had got himself in a little deeper than he wanted to be.

'What I mean is' – he sensed the prickly little person beside him – 'that your dad shared that idea of equality, but the other way round. I mean, he was very fair, like Henry, but not like Henry. If you see what I mean.'

No. I didn't. His meaning was about as clear as his handwriting on prescriptions. And I didn't like the taste of the medicine either.

'Och, but I'm havering now. You'd best get in and have your tea. Don't be late, in case Henry's feeling particularly egalitarian.'

I waved him off down the hill with the feeling that he had skirted round saying something quite unpleasant. However, I decided to give him the benefit of the doubt, as doubt was something of which I had plenty to spare.

In the kitchen Henry remarked on the dual misfortune, as he saw it, of both flat tyre and MacIntyre.

'I hope you're not going to make a habit of it?'

'Having punctures?'

'No, riding around with MacIntyre. Look at what it did to your father. Turned him into a raving sub-medical missionary.'

I thought very carefully before risking a reply.

'Doctor MacIntyre doesn't think so.'

'MacIntyre doesn't think, full stop. But what doesn't he think in particular?'

'That it was him that made my father the way he was.'

'What, a do-gooding buffoon?'

'Well, yes. He thinks it has something to do with you.'

An astonished smile creased Henry's face. He lifted his eyebrows.

'With me? He does, does he? And how did he come to that absurd conclusion?'

'I'm not really sure. Something to do with you both being egalitarian or something . . .'

'Hmm.' Henry continued to eat his supper. After a while he spoke again thoughtfully. 'You know, he may just have a point there. For once. Perhaps beneath that raucous sawbones' thick skull there lurks an almost functional brain. You see, I have, in my time, been patronised by those of a liberal leaning who theorise that misanthropes are merely disillusioned idealists. Absolute rubbish of course but . . .' He paused for another mouthful and chewed over what he was thinking. 'I do believe that MacIntyre may have come up with a new and far more interesting slant. It's a chicken and egg situation. Everyone assumes that the right-minded cynic, like my own fair self, is a poisoned idealist, unable to bear the burden of guilt of all mankind. But no!' He brandished his fork in mock triumph. 'The idealist, the world-saving do-gooder like your father is merely a misguided misanthrope!'

This was all passing over my head, but Henry was thoroughly enjoying himself, his smile growing between mouthfuls. The triumph in his voice grew more genuine by the minute.

'Now then, someone like myself sees humanity as one great faceless mass, barely worth the effort of differentiating into individual units, and whole-heartedly condemns it as such. They, however, the idealists, see it exactly the same way, the only difference being that they feel some perverse urge to scrape it up off the pavement and make it better!' Henry laughed loud and long 'So, perhaps MacIntyre is right. I am to blame for your father. I must pray for forgiveness.'

This made me angry. I didn't like his tone and I did not like what he might have been implying. Whatever that was.

'But my father didn't do anything wrong. He did his best to . . .'

'Yes, yes, I know,' he interrupted impatiently. 'He performed all his wondrous good deeds. And look where that got him. A valiant struggle it may well have been, but utterly pointless. What use is there in dragging those at the bottom of the heap, where at least they enjoy a little instinctive struggling, to the same level of abject mediocrity as the rest of us, leaving them bumbling around in the same no man's land . . .' He snorted crossly, then rose to clear the table.

'Anyway, there's no point in getting excited about it now, no point in wearing our hearts out. Not when real help is at hand.' He smiled. 'Fear not. For redemption cometh.' His finger was raised dramatically but wilted with his voice.

'Yes. Redemption cometh.'

He spoke very quietly, then was gone.

twenty-four

In which we receive a warning

I ascribed Henry's peculiar mood to the after-effects of his funny turn and kept safely out of the way until he had perked up a bit. After a couple of days he brightened a little and began to speak once more at meals.

'You seem to be hanging round the house a lot boy,' he said at breakfast. 'Shouldn't you be out further expanding the frontiers of geographical understanding?'

I treated him to one of my more vacant expressions.

'The bicycle, boy. You haven't been out exploring on it.'

'Oh, yes. Well, no, I haven't. I got a puncture.'

'Haven't you repaired that yet?'

'Well, er, no . . .'

'There's a repair kit in the shed.'

'Oh. Good.' I feigned enthusiasm.

'Assuming, that is, you know how to use one.'

'Ah. Well . . .'

'I thought as much. Incompetent child,' he muttered, and, as he polished off his breakfast declared, 'then I think it's about time that you learned, isn't it?'

'Yes. I suppose it is.'

'Right. Be by the shed in half an hour.' Henry went off to the study and I returned to my room to wait.

At the given hour I was standing by the shed, watching the chickens parade in the sun. Oscar sat nearby, feigning a lack of interest in this small army of mobile dinners, probably because he knew that any approach to the wire would lead to his instant reduction to cat paté. After a few minutes Henry emerged from the house carrying a basin of water. He set it down on the grass beside me then opened the shed door. I wheeled the bike out while he searched around for the puncture repair kit.

'Here we are, boy. Now then, invert the machine and we can set about taking this wheel off.'

The nuts put up some resistance, but were duly detached and lifted from the forks. Henry made it all look very easy as he levered off the tyre with the aid of two old spoons. He provided a running commentary as he ran through the various stages, inflating the inner tube, running it through the water, looking for the telltale bubbles. The hole was patched and left to dry before the wheel was reassembled.

'There we are,' said Henry, wiping his hands, 'you can replace the wheel now. But make sure that the nuts are tightened properly lest you should find yourself on a unicycle.'

I pumped up the tyre. Henry watched quietly, then began to speak.

'You know, guilt is not something that usually troubles me a great deal, but right now I'm sure that it's beginning to get the better of me. I feel a certain shame in being part of that terrible adult conspiracy, where children are expected to know everything that their seniors have had forty or fifty years to acquire whilst pretending all along that they knew it at your age. I think teachers must be the worst culprits."Oh, come along, surely you must know that" etc. You know the thing.'

I did and I smiled.

'In this particular case,' he continued, 'I am thinking of my own first attempts at cycle repair, when I carefully levered off the tyre with a screwdriver then wondered why the inner tube wouldn't inflate, until I found the neat little row of gashes all round the circumference. Of course, it was Robert who had to repair it in the end. He was always getting me out of pickles and' – he changed course rapidly – 'anyway, it just goes to show that anyone can make mistakes. We all have to learn some time.'

I was, as usual, intrigued by this mention of another name from the past, but any mystery that it might generate was immediately eclipsed by a far more incredible vision.

'You mean, you can ride a bicycle?' I asked. Even the adolescent doubts about the possibility of one's own conception by one's parents fade into insignificance when compared to the thought of an older relative on a bicycle. Henry looked down his nose and pulled himself up to his full height.

'Do you dare to cast aspersions on your old uncle's abilities? I, boy, am a renaissance man, well-versed in all the nobler arts, including the riding of the velocipede.'

Nor was Henry prepared to settle for this mere verbal assertion. He took a couple of paces over to where I stood and, with remarkable grace and speed, had righted the bicycle in a single movement. The saddle came to not far above his knee, but this did not deter him. Pausing only for another 'I'll show you' look down his nose, he bestraddled the machine in a great kinetic jumble of joints, his knees sticking out like those of a grasshopper. Like the outsized pistons of some primitive locomotive his legs began to propel him around the lawn, elbows raised to avoid the pumping knees. In and out of the trees and all round the lawn he pedalled, looking not unlike a circus chimp. He had gathered quite a bit of speed when he took his feet off the pedals and careered around the lawn, legs akimbo. What would have been an impressive enough end to the display was rendered positively spectacular by Henry's left foot, which chose to engage itself in a corner of the raspberry nets. The foot remained where it was, but the rest of Henry continued, like some huge pair of compasses, to describe a vast arc round the fulcrum of the tangled shoe, ending after about 150 degrees in a large heap amidst the neat rows of runner beans and sprouts.

I fell silent, momentarily worried about the possibility of

damage. And Henry might be hurt too. He lay quite still, then began to emit a low snorting sound, which turned into a heavy, wheezing breath, then erupted into gales of guffaws as Henry rolled himself onto his back and lay amidst the tangle of metal and greenery, laughing at the sky. Tears were rolling across his face by the time the footsteps sounded on the gravel. The large figure of Doctor MacIntyre came bounding across the lawn.

'My God. What's happened?' he cried in obvious alarm. It would have taken more than that to get any sense out of either of us. I pointed in dumb explanation at the wreckage of Henry as he lay back trying to gulp in air between great wheezing cackles. MacIntyre stood for a while, arms folded, failing to see the joke.

'When you are quite finished,' he said.

Henry was still laughing when he hauled himself, with my help, to a sitting position.

'What in God's name have you been doing, Henry?'

'I,' Henry snorted, 'have been repairing a puncture. And a few other things besides. I have been remembering and forgetting. But mostly, I have been repairing a puncture.' Then he was lost again for a minute or two, slapping up tiny dust clouds with his hand and turning even redder than he had managed for the doctor's last visit.

'Repairing a puncture eh?' I got the feeling that the doctor was not entirely convinced.

'Yes, MacIntyre, and at the same time demonstrating my aptitude, undiminished by the years, for falling off bicycles. An aptitude which kept one of your predecessors extremely busy.'

'And which will be keeping *me* busy if you're not careful, you old fool,' retorted the doctor. 'I thought I told you to rest.'

'But I am! Here I lie, relaxing in the sun-drenched comfort of my own vegetable patch.'

'Well, when you have quite finished relaxing, you can get up off your bum, because I want to talk to you.'

Henry, after one or two relapses, eventually made it to his feet and led us into the kitchen, where he began to fill the kettle.

'I'm not staying, this is a brief visit.'

'Oh good,' enthused a still giggly Henry.

'A visit with two purposes,' continued MacIntyre. 'One was to check that you are on the mend, which you plainly don't deserve to be . . .'

'Oh, so what?' cried Henry. 'At a time like this it would be like a man in front of a firing squad worrying about catching a chill.'

'Well, that's as may be, but the other reason for my visit is to deliver a warning.'

'Against what?'

'That I'm not sure about, but I thought I should let you know that Murchie, and some of your other fans, are up to something, something which I'm sure concerns you. And whatever it is, I don't like the smell of it.'

'Oh, I don't think we need to worry about him, MacIntyre. He's already been up here to pester me once, and I soon saw him off. I rather enjoyed it really.'

'Yes, I'm sure you did, but this is something different, something a bit more sophisticated. As I said, I'm not quite sure what they're up to, but I'll keep an ear to the ground.'

'My vegetable patch is very comfortable for that sort of thing . . .'

'Be serious Henry. Just keep your eyes open, that's all.'

'All right. Jolly good of you to let me know.'

'And another thing, Henry,' the doctor added wearily, 'no more circus tricks. Please?'

Henry nodded earnestly and promised to be good. MacIntyre nodded doubtfully and left without further comment.

As soon as he had gone we smiled the smiles of the half-chastened and returned to some semblance of normality, while Henry quietly abused MacIntyre and the medical profession in general.

twenty-five

❧

In which we receive a mysterious visitor

Henry's one-man circus performance signalled the start of the most tolerable, and even enjoyable, part of my stay at Halfway House so far. No one seemed more amused by the whole business than Henry himself, especially as he had finally managed to annoy the usually impervious MacIntyre.

'Did you see his face, boy? Lolloping across the lawn on a mission of mercy! Must have thought that my heart had gone again – as opposed to my head. It gave me immense satisfaction seeing that unflappable veneer crack for once. He's so tremendously thick-skinned – needs to be, I suppose, to keep the rest of him in – and will only respond to abuse by either laughing or replying in what he likes to think of as equal terms. But this time we got him!'

'I think he was quite worried,' I ventured in a more serious tone.

'Worried? Nonsense. He hasn't got the sense to worry. If there's one thing I can't abide it's gratuitous jollity. Especially as purveyed by MacIntyre.'

Despite having stated his case against gratuitous jollity, Henry allowed himself a triumphant chuckle. 'It's about time the smile was wiped off his face.'

The most rigorous scrubbing would have been useless in trying to remove the smile from Henry's face. It went with the almost mischievous humour which accompanied him for several days. He even suggested a trip to the local shop for a spot of villager-baiting, but decided against it on the grounds that he was due for a visit to Inverness soon.

I found it very difficult to account for this lightening of Henry's spirits. My only guess was that the war was now unavoidably close and that the joy of anticipation had got the better of him. However, there was little evidence to back this up. I heard nothing on the wireless, and Henry never mentioned the approach of Armageddon. There had to be some other reason. Perhaps the trouble with his heart had affected his brain as well. His behaviour was eccentric enough at the best of times, perhaps he had just slipped a little further . . . Whatever the reason, I definitely preferred Henry in this mood, and it was with a certain trepidation that I awoke one morning to a silent boiler. It was another disappearing day, and I was sure that it would undermine Henry's buoyancy, that he would come home sad and subdued as usual, taking us back to square one. I lay back in bed to show the ceiling my disappointment.

Outside, there continued a summer so glorious that it must have got lost while migrating south. As I did every morning, I opened the curtains expecting the great blue bubble of sky to have burst. But no, every morning it just beamed back and chided me for still being indoors. Such liberal supplies of sunshine are not to be wasted, so I decided that this would be the day when I relaunched the bicycle. If, that was, I could manage to ride it without collapsing into a helpless heap, paralysed with mirth at the vision of Henry's virtuoso performance. I reckoned that I would just manage, even vowing to take the puncture repair kit and practice my newly acquired mechanical skills should the need arise. But first there was the small matter of breakfast and lunch, so I dressed in my usual slapdash fashion and proceeded to the kitchen. Henry must have assumed that I knew the drill by now, because the note on the table merely read

Gone out etc.,
Henry

I set about the etc, slicing cheese for sandwiches while the toast
burned. The picnic parcel was tied, ready for the bike basket,
breakfast was eaten and plate and cup washed up, then I was off
across to the shed, stopping only to tease Oscar with a piece of
grass. He was distracted by a bird, so I continued across the lawn to
the shed. I put the sandwiches in the basket, along with the
puncture repair kit and the old spoons. It didn't occur to me to take
a spanner as well, but I did have the faithful map and a couple of
very nice tomatoes. I wheeled my steed down the garden and was
just passing the back door when it occurred to me that I had no
money with me. I had left it all in a neat pile on the desk. It would
be unwise to risk passing an ice cream shop without being properly
prepared, so I ran quickly upstairs to my room. I was just nearing
the top of the first flight, bounding up the steps in pairs, when there
was a heavy knock on the front door. I stopped dead, legs spread
over three stairs in a position that was far from comfortable if used
in a dramatic halt. The knocker sounded again and I turned and
began to walk slowly back down the stairs. I reached out to open
the door, but Dr MacIntyre's voice rang in my head – 'They're up
to something . . . up to something . . . up to . . .' I made it echo a
bit to add to the dramatic effect. There was another loud knock. I
wavered. Perhaps there was one thing worse than being found here
– not being found here. If they thought that the house was empty
then . . . Footsteps began to recede from the door. I dived across
and yanked it open.

'Yes. Who is it?' My voice, despite all attempts to the contrary,
was very shaky. The man in the grey suit turned from the course he
had set towards a blue car parked beyond the hedge.

'Ah, so there is someone in. Mr Dundas?'

'No, I'm his nephew.'

'I mean, where is Mr Dundas?' He looked and sounded official.
Had he come any closer I'm sure he would have smelled official.

'He's out,' I said.

'Out?'

146

'Yes. Out. Not in.'

'I see. When will he be back.'

'Not until later today.'

'And you're here by yourself?'

'Yes. Until he gets back this afternoon.'

'I see. Well then, I shall have to call back another day.'

'Can I take a message or anything?'

'No, no, I'll come back.' He turned away and it was not until the car had started and moved off down the hill that I closed the door and stood with my back to it (I was rather fond of this position). Dr MacIntyre was right. They were up to something. What is more, they were up to it on our very doorstep.

I knew that the day would be unbearably long if I waited at home for Henry. I had to keep myself occupied. Official-looking people are always disturbing. There was something in the back of my mind that was able to distinguish between absurd paranoia and the scent of real trouble. Unfortunately, it wasn't decent enough to inform the front of my mind of this important distinction, but satisfied itself by allowing vague signals to percolate through with hints that 'You thought you had something to worry about before! Well, just wait . . .' My subconscious insisted on following me around all day, worrying away without mercy through the deserted roads. There was still nobody about, even at the height of the holiday season. They were all at home, worrying about the war. But then, they hadn't met the man in the grey suit.

Later that afternoon, on my way down the hill as I headed home, I was overtaken by the bus, which grumbled past half-choking me with fumes. I pedalled furiously to catch up but there were not enough gears to make this worthwhile, so I gave up and coasted the rest of the way, pulling up at the junction to check for any other traffic. I was just about to push off when I saw the familiar figure of Henry striding round the corner. I cycled towards him.

'Hello,' I called cheerily.

'Oh, there you are, boy. Home is this way in case you had forgotten.' He seemed a little deflated, but not as completely subdued as he had been in the past. I wheeled round, jumped off and walked beside him.

'No punctures today, boy?'

'No.'

'Go far?'

'Not very.'

We passed the manse. I was waiting for the best moment to break the news to him. Instead I decided to try cheering him up.

'Something quite funny happened here.'

'Oh?'

'Remember the day that you were ill?'

'I remember it extremely well. A little short on hilarity as I recall.'

'No, not that. But when I cycled down for help . . .'

'I hope this isn't going to be one of MacIntyre's stories. If so I don't want to hear it.'

'No. It was before I reached him.'

'Good.'

'Well, I was coming down the hill very quickly, and across the bridge, pedalling like mad, and he, er, Mr Murchie that is, came out of that gate. There wasn't enough time to stop or swerve or anything so I just kept going and he had to dive backwards. He fell into a flowerbed when the gate opened behind him. He was ever so cross and it looked ever so funny . . .'

Henry stopped in his tracks and looked round sternly.

'Do you mean to say that you nearly ran over a minister of the Church of Scotland?'

'Well, yes, I . . .' I was quite taken aback.

'Well yes nothing. It's just not good enough. Miss another opportunity like that and I'll take both your wheels off and hide them.' I sighed. You never quite knew with Henry.

'On the other hand,' Henry continued, striding off again, 'actual physical collision with something as slimy as Murchie hardly bears thinking about.'

I said nothing else until we reached the house, where I noticed that the front door had a 'Haven't you told him yet' look about it. I put the bike away and met Henry in the kitchen where he was feeding a noisy Oscar.

'By the way,' I said.

'Yes?'

'A man came to the door today.'

'Really?'

'A man with a grey suit.'

'I hope you told him that I never wear grey.'

'No, he was wearing the suit.'

'Oh, I see. Not wearing a uniform?'

'No.'

'Hadn't come to read a meter or something?'

'I don't think so. He didn't say why he had come. But he asked for you.'

Henry turned to look at me.

'Did he leave any kind of message?'

'No. He just said that he would be back, then drove off.'

'How peculiar,' mused Henry, filling the kettle. 'Probably trying to sell something, I should imagine.'

'I don't know. He looked sort of official.'

'Perhaps he came to explain how to pay one's rates in the event of the apocalypse.'

Henry seemed unconcerned, but I wanted some reassurance.

'I was a bit worried.'

'Why's that boy?'

'It's just that Dr MacIntyre said that someone was up to something and . . .'

'Pah. What does he know. I'm sure it was just one of his puerile practical jokes. Trying to worry us, that's all. Don't let it bother you, then we'll have the last laugh.'

Even in my darkest and most fearful hours I had admired Henry for his unassailable tact-free honesty. But now, when he was saying just what I wanted to hear, I wasn't so sure . . .

twenty-six

In which the mysterious visitor returns

It was just after breakfast, a couple of days later, when the blue car drew up outside again. I could see it from my bedroom window and watched with a renewed sense of trepidation as the same grey suit walked officially over the gravel to knock officially on the door. I came out of my room and down one flight of stairs, just as Henry opened the front door. I stayed where I was, out of sight but able to hear what was going on.

'Yes?' said Henry. I could hear the look that he gave the man.

'Mr Henry Dundas?'

'That is correct. And you must be the man in the grey suit.' This unbalanced him briefly.

'I, yes . . . I have come to deliver this to you.'

'Why? Post Office on strike, are they?'

'No. It is to be delivered in person.'

'What is it?'

'That will be perfectly clear when you open it.'

'What if I don't want it?'

'Take it please,' said the man, sounding especially official.

'Why should I if I don't know what it is? For all I know it could be the black spot.'

The grey suit was further bemused.

'No, it's a . . .' He caught himself in time.

'A what?'

'That will be perfectly clear when you open it.' He obviously hadn't been trained to deal with Henrys.

'I'm sorry, but if I don't know what it is why should I want to take it? In fact, I'm quite sure that I don't want to take it. I don't know you. I don't even like you. What's more, you're wearing a grey suit.' There was a short silence. 'With matching shoes,' Henry snorted. 'Now be a good chap and go away.'

The door slammed. A muffled voice cried from outside and knocked loudly. The door was yanked open.

'You don't understand, Mr Dundas.' He sounded a bit cross.

'NO. *You* don't understand Mr Dundas. Mr Dundas says go away, but you are still here, indicating an alarming inability to comprehend even the simplest of demands . . .'

Henry's patience seemed to be waning.

'Yes, but . . .'

'But nothing!'

Grey suit rapidly starched himself with renewed officialdom.

'If you do not take this now then I will return. If it is still not accepted then you will be forced to attend.'

There was a long silence. I waited for Henry's next outburst, but it didn't come. The door closed and I heard the car drive off. Henry went into the study, slamming the door behind him. He remained there for some time. I did not disturb him, partly because I was nervous of doing so, but more because I was in no hurry to hear what I was sure would be bad news. So, instead, I went upstairs to my room and waited. For what, I did not know, but I waited all the same.

I was sitting at the desk, doodling aimlessly and staring out across the glen, when the eerie silence was broken. Judging by what I could hear it was not the only thing being broken. I looked here and there out of the window, trying to pin down this peculiar racket of grunts and thuds. I could see nothing. The garden was empty. There was no one round the front either, but then the sound was most definitely coming from the garden or thereabouts. I looked again. The shed door was open. Surely Henry wasn't cycling again? No, he wasn't.

Above the wall the top of a pine tree was shuddering rhythmically, quaking between thud and grunt. He isn't, is he? Yes. He was . . .

'Henry!' I cried as I rounded the wall. He looked up briefly, then ignored me. The axe came swinging round again with an angry grunt. Splinters flew. The grunts were turning to war cries, the blows to murder.

'EEEAAH!' THUD . . . then another, then with one almighty swing and a lung-rearranging yell the tree began to creak. Then crack and creak in a great swooshing arc to land with a bounce and a rustle of limbs amongst the bracken. Flies and dust filled the air. Henry stood, wide-eyed, panting, his teeth clamped tight. The tree lay flat, wondering what it had done to upset him.

'Henry,' I called again.

'Yes, boy?' he replied as calmly as his heaving chest would allow.

'What are you doing?'

He looked down at his prostrate victim, then at me.

'Felling a tree, boy.'

'But you were told . . . I mean, last time it nearly . . .'

'Last time it was nearly finished. Now it is.' He lay the axe across his shoulder and walked past me. I scrambled after him.

'But, Henry . . .'

'You ought to know by now, boy, that I hate anything that is only half-done.'

He strode off at full speed. I ran to keep up as he turned into the garden and continued across the lawn to the shed. I waited for him to close the door and come back towards the house.

'Are you all right?'

'Yes,' he snapped.

'You look very red . . .'

'The heat.'

I followed him into the kitchen, where he stopped to fill a glass with water. He stood sipping it and staring out of the window.

'Who was he?'

'Who was what?' He rinsed the glass.

'The man at the door.'

'That was your friend in the grey suit.'

'What did he want?'

152

'Nothing.'

Henry disappeared into the study. I half followed him, but decided to give him some time to cool down. I filled the kettle and waited for it to boil. Then, armed with nothing but a cup of tea, I knocked on the study door.

'What is it?'

'It's me.' There followed a silence. 'Can I come in?' Another silence. Well, he hadn't said no, so I gingerly opened the door, expecting to be pinned to the wall by an angry yell.

'I made you some tea.'

'Thank you.' Henry lay stretched out on the settee, staring rue-fully at the ceiling. He was obviously suffering from the effects of his wood-cutting activities and pulled himself up with difficulty. He took the tea and sat it on the table beside him, saying nothing. I sat down.

'Are you sure you're all right?'

'Yes, boy, I'm fine.'

'You don't want me to call for . . .'

'MacIntyre? Good God no. I've had quite enough in the way of visitors today.' He picked up the tea and sipped.

'Who was that man?'

'Some petty official.' This was little help.

'What did he want?'

Henry set aside his tea and lay back again. Something of his usual dramatic tone returned.

'He came, boy, to rescue you.'

'Me?'

'Yes. He came to save you from the clutches of your evil old uncle.'

'I don't understand. I thought he was trying to give you something.'

'So you heard, eh?' Henry stared accusingly.

'Well, yes . . .' I confessed quietly.

'Yes, you're right. He was trying to give me something. It's a letter from the courts. My custody of you has been challenged as unsuitable.'

'But by who?'

'By whom, boy.'

'By whom then?'

Henry returned to his tea and added to the suspense.

'Well,' he said at last, 'Murchie seems to have had something to do with it. And that awful Calder woman.'

'Aunt Margaret?'

'The very same.'

'But I wrote and told her that I was quite happy here,' I protested. I had told her that. All right, so it had been a lie at the time, but it was what I had told her.

'That's all very well, but I'm sure Murchie's twisted mind and minimal grasp of logic will soon account for that minor abberation. He will merely assume that you have either been intimidated or corrupted, and that your letter was proof of one or the other.'

'But it's true.'

'What's true?'

'I am quite happy here . . .' Henry fell silent then muttered impatiently –

'Yes, yes. All right, boy. Just think yourself lucky. Now we can both get on with what remains of our lives in peace. You won't have to put up with my misanthropic rantings and I won't have to put up with you rampaging up and down my stairs and drinking all my orange juice.'

'But I . . .'

'But nothing. Go on. Run along and enjoy your last days of imprisonment in Castle Dundas.' He rose and walked over to one of the book cases, pulled out a book and pretended to read it. I sat where I was, beginning to suffer from acute condensation of the eyeballs. I sniffed involuntarily.

'Henry?'

'I'm trying to read, boy. Off you go.' I scuffed to the door at a funereal pace and pulled it open.

'Henry?'

'What is it, boy' His voice was impatient and his back remained towards me.

'Why did you chop the tree down? This morning?'

The book thudded shut. 'Because, boy' he turned, 'I did not have Murchie to hand. Now run along.' He pointed to the door and I left with the faintest smile of hope clinging to my face.

twenty-seven

✿

The day of reckoning approaches

My time in the Highlands was tapering to an end in an ever-narrowing wedge. Its broad end was the nightmare of the first few days, swollen and protracted under a magnifying glass of trepidation, when every cautious word echoed and every movement was in self-conscious slow motion. Then, hours would drag by. But now, as I grew to accept, and even, I had to admit, quite enjoy life here, time slipped past even quicker. And the faster it slipped past the more sure I was that I would miss it all. As my small history shot by me I grabbed at it, but still it slipped away, faster and faster, leaving my grasping fingers burning like the pain in my lungs as I panted and pedalled my way round the summer roads, desperately gulping at what was left. The harder I gulped the more I spilled until, very soon, that summer week was lost, as irretrievable as an ice cream dropped on hot tarmac. There was only one thing to do.

I moped.

Henry remained quite bluff about the whole affair, pointing out how convenient the timing of the court appearance was, as he was due for a trip to Inverness anyway. I failed to see any lighter side and sat with a drooping face at the breakfast table, only a day away from doom.

'Oh, cheer up, boy. It's not all that bad. Look on the bright side. We might be about to go down in history.'

'Why's that?' I grunted with the minimum of interest.

'Well, just think, with the world about to be extinguished at any moment this could well be the last will ever to be challenged!' He roared with laughter at this but my lip remained firmly at half mast.

'I hope it is blown up,' I muttered.

'What's that?'

'I said I hope it is blown up. The world. I'm sick of it.'

'Oh dear,' said Henry, 'perhaps I *have* been corrupting you after all.' He smiled.

'It's just not fair,' I moped on. 'First Father . . . and now this.'

'But you'll soon be free of all this,' Henry gestured around him.

'You know what I mean. I mean . . .'

'Yes?'

'I mean . . . I don't want to go,' I mumbled quickly.

'Oh, don't be stupid, boy.'

'Well I don't. I don't want to go.'

Henry stared quizzically over the top of his tea cup.

'As I recall,' he mused, 'And do correct me if I'm wrong, not so long ago you were trying to run away.'

My jaw overtook my bottom lip.

'No I didn't,' I protested loudly, 'And anyway, how did you know?'

'Because I saw you scampering up the hillside as if all the hounds of hell were after your tail. Hiding in the copse then bolting out like a frightened rabbit.'

'But I thought . . .'

'How do you think I knew where to find you?'

'Well, I . . . sorry.'

We finished eating and I helped Henry to clear the table. He washed and I dried.

'Will I have to go back to Edinburgh?'

'You make it sound like Siberia!'

'It's worse. They don't have Aunt Margaret in Siberia.'

'I'm sure it could be arranged.'

I allowed one small giggle before continuing with my mope.

'I hate the city. It's so big and noisy and . . .'

'Full of people,' added Henry with disgust. 'Yes, I quite agree, boy, there is little joy to be found in the prospect of returning to the gum-pocked concrete of the metropolis, but, needs must.'

'It's so much more interesting here, with the hills and everything. I'll miss all that.'

Henry was quiet as the last of the cutlery was dried and the drawer closed.

'How would you like,' he said, drying his hands, 'a trip across the hills?'

'But I thought that you said that I wasn't supposed to go up there ever again?'

'I said that you were never to go up there alone and unprepared. This time I will ensure that you are neither.'

'Oh?'

'I am proposing a guided tour with my own fair self providing any necessary guidance or commentary on the various sights and sounds. What do you think of that idea?'

'That would be great. Thank you!'

'Good. Provided that you promise to endeavour not to fall off, into or under anything, we shall set off at nine-thirty. Despite the extravagant promises of the weather forecast it would be wise to bring a jumper and a waterproof. Oh yes, and the map to be on the safe side. In the interests of dignity I will make the sandwiches.'

By nine-fifteen I was as organised as I would ever be and waited for Henry outside the back door. On the dot of half-past we set off up the hill, following the path that I had first taken onto the ridge. Henry's lack of faith in the weather forecast was ill-founded. Another glorious blue and green of a day embraced us as we wandered far into the hills. Henry didn't stop to consult the map once, he seemed to know the area intimately, disappearing down side tracks to point out minute details in the landscape, oddly shaped rocks, animal lairs and numerous places where he had come to grief as a boy. We saw the deer again, grazing in the distance, and Henry told me of their wild times in the rutting season when they would sometimes come down into the glen and occasionally wreak havoc.

'They grow very bold at that time of year. I remember one year when some youth from the village was riding around on a motor cycle. You know the sort of thing, where the amount of noise produced by the engine is in inverse proportion to its actual power and the I.Q. of the rider. Anyway, one particularly large stag which was foraging by the roadside heard this infernal machine roaring along towards him. Well, he regarded this as some sort of challenge and charged the youth as he went past. Caught him side on and knocked him clean off the machine.'

'Was he all right?'

'I think so. He went bounding back up the hill when he realised his mistake and found out that it wasn't another stag. Hardly surprising really. Have you ever seen a stag on a motor cycle?'

And so our trek continued in a respectful silence, broken only when Henry would point out some bird or animal. He knew the names of every one, and the full Gaelic title and nicknames of all the hills and mountains. He would come out with occasional anecdotes and legends of a most unlikely nature and, just sometimes, I was faintly reminded of Father's dubious tales. Maybe this was something else he had picked up from Henry.

In some ways it would have been better if Henry had been the frightening and obnoxious man I had first met at Halfway House. Maybe then the following day might not have seemed quite so ominous. Instead, so quietly tired and happy was I by the time we began our descent, that any possible reasons for wanting to leave, which might just have cushioned my fall, had melted away. As we neared the house I knew that tomorrow was just a day away (an astute observation) and my spirits sank down into my boots, turning my feet to lead as I trudged the final few hundred yards.

'Come along, boy, supper beckons.' Henry strode on ahead. I stopped for a minute, watching the long shadows stretch across the valley floor. And those rampaging butterflies had returned to my stomach. All seemed lost along that final stretch of sheep track.

How different supper was to what I had hoped was my last meal in Edinburgh. There, overjoyed by the prospect of imminent escape, I had had absolutely no trouble in articulating my sorrow at leaving in the most eloquent manner. But now, as I sat opposite Henry, I was as silent as those first few days at Halfway House. And all because I had so very much to say.

twenty-eight

In which, as usual, nothing goes to plan

Given my tender years I knew very little of the workings of the law, although I had managed to work one thing out for myself. If you were to have any chance of proving, in court, that you had not been abused or neglected, if you were to give the impression of being comfortable and civilised, and to show that you were mature enough to know as well as anyone what was in your own best interests, then it was probably best if you didn't smell. A bath was not only in order but extremely overdue.

Had I realised at the time just what sort of repercussions were to follow from that particular bath then I would have remained comfortably rancid and faced the consequences. However, at the time it seemed like a good idea so, with Henry's permission, the boiler was activated. I waited some time after supper before taking this dramatic step. I felt it wise to allow time to digest and thus avoid the risk of cramp, it never having dawned on me that it was the exertion and not just the immersion which made swimming a deadly post-prandial pursuit. Just before bedtime I lowered myself into the steamy tub and lay for a while watching a perfect blue strip at the top of the open window steadily darkening into night. I even went as far as washing, giving myself a thorough scrub until I emerged in a state of such radiant cleanliness that I was sure that any judge, or who so ever might be deciding my fate, would immediately recognise my intense spiritual welfare and throw the case out of court in a matter of seconds. Remarkably invigorating things, baths . . .

As I slid between the sheets much of my defeatism had been abandoned. I would fight. I would show them. I would stand up for my rights. I would never get to sleep if that wretched boiler didn't shut up soon. I had forgotten about the other after-effect of bathing at Henry's. The thing-behind-the-wardrobe had begun the night shift. It was conspiring with all the authorities, Murchies and Margarets to keep me awake and sap my strength. The harder I tried to get to sleep the wider awake I grew. Still it glurped and clanked. Had it been a cat I would have thrown a boot at it, but there was no way to scare this racket away. On and on it gurgled. I tossed and turned, blocked my ears, tried and tried to ignore it, but all to no avail. I pulled a pillow over my head but found that the habits of a lifetime are hard to break. Especially that of breathing. I don't know what time it was when I finally got to sleep, but things got no better when I did. It was a light and lukewarm slumber, full of twisted dreams that mingled themselves with the dark and solid furniture of the real room.

Outside on the wall Oscar had metamorphosed into a giant boiler cat, who sat baying at the mechanical moon, conducted by Murchie, Margaret, the man in the grey suit and a trio of Gilbert and Sullivan judges. The room was full of boots. I struggled with the window. The rubbery catch would not shift. I smashed it out and began to throw the boots, flinging them with all my strength, but they tugged against the air and drifted, like feathers, down into the garden. And the feathers turned to birds, singing above the wailing of the boiler cat, the siren wailing of the boiler cat as the sky grew bright. And this brightness was war, this brightness was welcomed by the birds with their false-dawn chorus. No. You mustn't believe it. It isn't the dawn. Run. Hide. The boiler cat was Oscar again. Run Oscar, run. Don't listen to the bird. Don't listen to the cuckoo. Cuckoo. Cuckoo!

Cuckoo! I sat bolt upright, as one is supposed to do when

160

wakening from nightmares. The boiler was now just muttering to itself, but there, there it was again. Cuckoo! I could not believe my ears. Here was a bird not satisfied with merely hijacking nests but intent on usurping the very dawn! No blackbird or thrush, no wren, not even that most incompetent of time-keepers, the cockerel, was to have the first word this morning. The dawn chorus was to follow the rhythm of this two note metronome. Cuckoo, cuckoo. And round it they came, mistier and mistier, all the birds of Inverness-shire. Every bloody one of them. Not to mention a few sheep and something which remained anonymous but sounded very much as if it was falling out of a tree. I plunged my head under the covers and groaned. Half-past four it was, and me so desperate for sleep. I cursed them and damned them, wished I had a gun, longed for some cotton wool, anything for some sleep. Eventually I just gave up the fight and resigned myself to a complete lack of rest. It was then that I nodded off again.

When the birds started up a second time I cursed them once more and shouted loudly –

'Go away!' To which they calmly replied –

'I do so admire those who can start the day so well.'

'Oh, sorry. I was asleep. Just . . .'

'I thought it best to waken you,' continued Henry, 'as we shall have to catch the early bus. Breakfast is ready when you are.'

Henry went back down the stairs and I sat on the edge of the bed, grinding away at my eyeballs. I yawned and shivered a bit. So this was it, the day of reckoning. It seemed that all my spirit of defiance had drifted away in the night, evaporating with my breath as I lay amidst the midnight racket. The sun, once again, failed to appreciate my plight and beamed down inanely from a sky streaked with early morning cloud. I shivered a bit more in the cold shade of the room and opened the wardrobe.

However much my spirits may have sagged I was still clean from my bath, but this was not enough in itself. I must be smart as well. I selected a clean pair of trousers with creases in the appropriate places. I wasn't overly fond of formal attire, but this was an emergency. A white shirt, and even a tie, a blazer, like my school one but clean, plus school shoes, given a thorough polish, and the outfit was complete. I admired myself in the mirror and concluded that, once I had got the shoe polish out of my finger nails, I would be ready to face the world.

I strode proudly into the kitchen and stood to attention with a small stamp. Henry looked round and stared with a wrinkled brow.

'Do I know you?'

'It's me!'

'Oh yes, so it is. I'm just not used to seeing you in clothes that don't look slept in.'

'I thought I would make an effort, just to show them that I'm all right. I don't look neglected, do I?'

'Not at the moment. But after breakfast might be a different matter. Here, use this.' Henry produced a napkin from a drawer by the sink. 'It might be wise to take off the jacket as well.'

We sat down to breakfast earlier than usual. Both of us remained fairly quiet and I found that my appetite was being impeded by the rampaging butterflies. After a while Henry's watch made an ominous appearance.

'Well, boy, this is it. We had best be going. Just leave the plates and we'll deal with them later.' Later was something that didn't bear thinking about.

We wasted no time in setting off down the hill. Henry passed a few comments on the weather and our surroundings but I kept quiet, silenced by nerves and the creeping tiredness that was the legacy of my noisy night. It was not until we reached the bridge that I felt the need to say anything. I stopped to watch the burn tumble past.

'Henry?'

'Come along, boy.'

'If I do have to go . . .'

'We'll miss the bus!' I ran after him.

'How old do you have to be before you can do what you want?'

Henry laughed. 'I very much doubt if that is an age which any of us ever reach!'

'You know what I mean. When you don't have to be in anyone's custody, as a child.'

'Well, eighteen I suppose. But at sixteen you can leave home. Even get married if you so desire.'

'Oh . . .' We continued down into the village.

'Henry?' I said at last.

'Yes, boy?'

'When I'm old enough . . .'

'Yes?'

'Can I come back again?'

'That,' he replied without looking round, 'is rather an academic question.'

'A what?'

'It means that there is little point in asking it, because, by the time you reach that age, I doubt if any of us will still be around.'

'Oh,' I said again. This reply was something of a disappointment, not because it implied the relatively unimportant end of the world, but because it hadn't really answered my question.

'Yes, but if we did live to be . . . I mean, could I?'

'Yes, boy. Now hurry up before that wretched charabanc leaves without us.'

We turned into the High Street, me revelling in this positive, if not exactly enthusiastic, answer. Henry strode on up to the bus and climbed aboard. The expected silence fell but it didn't seem to bother him in the least.

'One and a half to the station, please. Thank you.' His voice was loud, as if to emphasise the deadly hush, which he seemed to relish. The tickets whirred out of the driver's machine and Henry tucked them into his waistcoat pocket. Before sitting down beside me he stopped in the aisle, surveying both sides of the bus with careful distaste, then shaking his head sadly. The silence intensified until the driver started up, then, above the roar of the engine, conversation cautiously crept back.

None of it was between Henry and myself. We both remained quiet all the way to the station, where we were the only ones to alight. There was a gap of fifteen minutes before the train was due, so we waited on benches on the deserted platform.

'It shouldn't take long.'

'Hmm?'

'The journey to Inverness,' continued Henry. 'It shouldn't take long.'

'Oh.' We fell silent again. I watched a jackdaw strutting up and down one of the beams of the roof, as if performing some absurd music hall walk. There was nobody about. Henry broke the silence again.

'What shall we have for supper tonight?'

'Don't know.'

'We could always eat in Inverness. Wait around and do some shopping, then go for a meal somewhere.'

'I thought you hated towns?'

'I do. But it does so help in firming up the convictions. Anyway, we'll see how we feel.'

We waited some more. The adrenalin of early morning was beginning to fade. My collar felt tight and my shoes uncomfortable. I was painfully tired, that unpleasant filleted feeling that a lack of sleep induces, and was half dozing when the train arrived.

'Come along, boy.'

We climbed aboard and found a seat in an almost empty carriage. I watched the scenery pass without taking any of it in and only half heard anything that Henry said. The journey was not particularly long and was further foreshortened by the undesirability of the destination. We arrived on time and had soon passed through the station door and into the hot, busy square beyond. It seemed like a very long time since I had walked on streets full of people. Being shut away at Halfway House had left me oblivious to the tensions that had steadily risen here in the outside world. Newspaper headlines muttered darkly, faces were set in bleak concentration as we struggled through crowded parts of the pavement. We were jostled by the ill-tempered crowd. Car horns sounded angrily, and somewhere down the street a voice began to shout. The weather, which had once seemed like a parting gift, was now part of the torture. I was too hot and too tired. I wanted to be back at the house, sitting in the shade of the garden, in peace and quiet. But it was too late for that now. A whole window full of watches said ten o'clock. The end, as far as I was concerned, was already nigh.

'We had better hurry up,' said Henry looking around him at the crowd with the air of a man who has inadvertently found himself in a field full of cow pats. I followed him along the pavement, steadily switching off as I went. The traffic became a distant rumble, my eyes became glazed and perhaps just a little damp. I was in a world of my own by the time we came to the crossing. I had been staring vacantly at my reflection in a shop window, trying to weigh the sartorial importance of my collar and tie against the need for oxygen, when I realised that Henry was already crossing the road. The lights were changing when I dashed out from behind a fat man in a dirty white shirt. The car was going too fast to stop, impatiently cutting round the tail of the crossing pedestrians. I timed my leap into its path with unconscious perfection. The result was perfect unconsciousness. The road and the car came at me from all sides. The sky went spinning round and down past the kerb. A salty taste in my mouth and a chill rising up from my feet. The road was very near. Tiny flecks of silver danced in the tarmac. The world was huge but shrinking fast. They couldn't take me away now. I had already gone. And the world had gone. Only the tarmac was left, still dancing with silver until it too was eaten up by black. Everything had gone now. And there I lay, beneath the bumper of a foreign car that was forever dented.

twenty-nine

*In which death turns out to be
something of a disappointment*

I didn't really mind being dead. Not after last night. I needed the rest. It was nice and quiet and I was quite sure that nobody would disturb me. Did they have cuckoos in the after life? I doubted it, but still I could hear something singing, very far away. A steady rhythmic song of chirps, very far away.

It wasn't black any more. Now it was all white, with a hint of blue, and so very quiet. There was no boiler here, so now I could get to sleep. And that bird wouldn't disturb me. Not if it stayed so far away. It was so noisy in that street. So loud and angry. No wonder Henry hates people. So glad to be away from all that. Time to get some sleep. I'm so tired, I must sleep. I hate all that noise. Henry hates all the noise. And the people. He has to hurry now. To the court. But of course, he won't need to now. Because I'm dead . . . .

Henry in the court. Me dead. They'll blame Henry. But they mustn't. It was my fault. The stupid driver's fault. Not Henry's. They'll blame him. They mustn't, it's all . . .

'Oh dear. You're one of those, are you?' said an agitated voice. 'One of what?'

'What I call a clinger. A hanger-on. They always think they have some grand mission to complete and struggle back. I blame the cinema myself.'

'Who are you?'

'That is neither here nor there. And neither are you.'

He was a small man, thin and nervous, looking as if he was in a hurry. He wore a dark green suit with a matching tie and fussed over his pocket watch. Give him a pair of long ears and he would have made a perfect white rabbit.

'Where am I?' I asked.

'At this precise moment you are in hospital. What I want to know is whether you intend staying here.' He fidgeted with his watch again. 'Oh, this is bothersome. Now of all times to have to come across a clinger.'

'In hospital?'

'That is what I said,' he snapped impatiently.

'Are you a doctor then?' At this he began to laugh. Well, titter really.

'I have been called many things in my time – but never that! Oh, I must remember that one. Mind you, some doctors these days . . . anyway, I haven't got all day.'

'Sorry.'

'It's no good being sorry. You'll have to make up your mind.' He produced his watch again and a small black notebook. 'And soon if you don't mind.'

'Make up my mind about what?'

'Oh dear. Do I have to spell it out? You'll only get upset.'

'I don't understand,' I protested.

'What do people normally do when they are run over by a car. Apart from sue?'

'Well they . . .'

'Precisely. They die. But now, today, with everything else going on . . . I mean, any day now it could happen. And what do I get? A clinger. A can't make up his mind. Oh . . . bother.'

'Die? But I thought I already had.'

'Of course not, you stupid child. Otherwise I would have been here already.'

'You mean that you're . . .'

167

'Yes, that's right. Well done.'

'But I thought that . . .'

'Yes, yes, I know. Scythe, big hood and high cheekbones. And all black people have rhythm. How I hate ignorant preconceptions. Almost as much as clingers . . .' he muttered.

'Sorry! I didn't realise that I was doing anything.'

'Precisely. You're not doing anything. And I haven't much more time.'

'But, you're not really what I expected.'

'Nor are you,' he mumbled, glancing at his watch again.

'I thought you would be far more . . . well, frightening.'

'But I am. There is nothing that scares the life, pardon the joke, out of your average self-important corpse as much as coming face to face with me. Because I'm so ordinary. When they realise that they're not even worth the hooded skull routine it does them more good than an eternity and a half in hell-fire would ever do.'

He stopped and adopted a sterner tone. 'Anyway, stop sidetracking me. This is your last chance.'

'To die?'

'Yes.'

'But, you see, I have to . . .'

'Right, that does it. I'm off. I just hope there aren't too many more like you around.'

'What, clingers?'

'Yes, clingers. It's bad enough with your average cadaver. "Do you know my husband Fred? Came to you oh, it must be fifteen years ago now . . ." As if I remembered them all. Do you know just how many people die in a day?' He seemed rather agitated.

'Well it isn't my fault,' I said.

'Not entirely. Anyway, I must get on. I just hope the next one is more cooperative.'

'Sorry to waste your time.'

'Sorry to disappoint you with my plain appearance,' he added, a little sarcastically I thought.

'That's all right . . .'

He headed for the door.

'You use doors?' I exclaimed.

168

'For heaven's sake, child! Will you let me get on. What do you expect me to do? Fade to a grin like the Cheshire cat?'

'Funny you should say that.'

'Why?'

'Well, I was just thinking that you remind me of the White Rabbit.'

'Don't mention rabbits,' he snapped. 'If there's one thing worse than clingers, it's rabbits. Can't keep the wretched things down. Dispose of one and another three appear in its place. Dreadful things. Breed like . . .'

'Rabbits?'

'Precisely. Now GOODBYE.' He set off purposefully, head down.

'By the way . . .'

'What is it now?'

'It's a nice suit.'

'Oh. Thank you.' He smiled. 'I mean, imagine actually wearing the hood and cloak and so on. Where would you keep your watch? No, I wouldn't be seen . . . Oh Lord! Just look at the time. Not another word.'

He was gone. Everything was black again. Sometimes it drifted between black and a deep, dark red. After some time, I have no idea how long, it began to fade to a light grey. It was then that the pains began. In my leg, my right leg, and my head. A throbbing, dull pain which would suddenly stab sharply with a burst of light, flashing white against the dark background. Then they too faded. For three days and nights I lay there, but to me it could have been hours, or minutes, or even years. All I was aware of was grey. Endless grey and dull pains. Then, around the third or fourth day, I became aware of something else. Someone was in the room. I knew they were there, although I could see and hear nothing. I just knew that someone was there. They were coming towards me, approaching the top of the bed. Maybe it was him! He had changed his mind. Perhaps I wasn't such a clinger after all. I waited for that fidgety voice, but it didn't come. There was another voice, a long way off, as if echoing down a very long toilet roll. A most familiar voice, which sighed and said,

'Stupid boy. What shall we do with you?' Then it sighed again. It was Henry. He was by the bed. I hoped that he wasn't too cross but he said nothing else. All I was aware of was a slight movement, as of something touching the pillow, then I could no longer sense anyone in the room. But there was something there. The vague impressions which had provided my sole tenuous link with the outside world now gave way to the first real sense. The sense of smell, triggered by that warm and slightly musty scent. Sawdust and fur. A smell as old as I was. It was coming from beside me on the pillow. Yes. It was the bear.

thirty

❦

*In which I return to the land
of the living*

Any chance that I may have had to die early and beat the rush had been forfeited due to my indecision and habit of talking too much. The far from grim Reaper was obviously a busy man and not one who took kindly to having his time wasted. This left no alternative other than recovery.

My return to the land of the living was a peculiar experience, a sensation not unlike the emptying of my bedroom sink. The water would tremble slightly then begin to sink imperceptibly before being grasped by greedy gulps and hauled gurgling into the darkest recesses of the waste pipe, leaving nought but a dirty grey ring and a glug glug glug. On the third metaphorical glug my eyes opened suddenly. They blurred and fluttered as though full of soap then focused on the ceiling. Then, having wakened themselves up they gave the ears a quick prod and they in turn focused on the sound of footsteps on linoleum. The nose was just beginning to recoil from the primary school and sick smell of disinfectant when a face, surmounted by an absurd hat, interposed itself between me and the ceiling, which I had been examining with an interest that it barely deserved. The face, still a pink blur, spoke.

'Hello.'

'Yes,' I replied quietly. Not quite the usual response but at least positive.

'Hello,' the pink blur repeated in a gentle female voice. It was beginning to organise itself into a proper face, with headgear that suggested a nurse.

'Where am I?'

'In the hospital,' she said, 'We've been very worried about you.'

'Oh. Where's Henry?'

'Henry?'

'My uncle. Where is he?'

'He went for a walk a little while ago. He should be back soon. Now just lie quietly and I'll call the doctor.' I heard the door flap shut behind her.

I nearly lay quietly, but curiosity got the better of me and I felt the need to look around. During my short sojourn in limbo my head had apparently put on a great deal of weight and resisted all but the most strenuous leverings of my stiff neck. I prised it up far enough to take in part of the clinically white room and the hint of sun coming through the blinds. There were a chair and locker by the bed and a stand from which there trailed tubes. Tubes which led to . . . My arm. There were tubes in my arm. My head sank into the pillow and my stomach into the bed springs. Being run over I could take. Death I could handle. I could even cope with meeting the Grim Reaper himself. That was all fine. But tubes . . . I was just reaching my most verdant hue when the nurse returned, accompanied by a young doctor.

After greeting me with what Henry would quite rightly have described as gratuitous jollity he set about giving me a thorough examination – peering into my eyes, checking pulses and breathing, prodding all the places that hurt most and generally making me feel far worse than I had done when he started. Once he had twisted, poked and peered to his satisfaction he pronounced me well-as-could-be-expected and really rather lucky. I didn't feel particularly lucky.

'You had a very close shave,' he said. 'We thought you were a goner when you were unconscious for so long. Lost your pulse once or twice as well, but you seem to have come out of it remarkably well considering. Mind you, one of your legs will be a bit painful' – a bit?! – 'as you managed to twist, sprain, fracture, you name it – everything except a nice clean break. There's also a bit of bruising on your head, it took a nasty knock, but it seems to be OK.'

172

'Hardly surprising is it, boy? Nothing much to damage up there.'

'Henry!' I cried.

'I'm sorry, sir,' the doctor said, 'visiting time isn't until . . .'

'Nonsense, man. Besides, I'm not a visitor, I have virtually been living here.'

'Yes, I realise that but . . .'

'Don't worry. I won't get in the way of whatever you're pretending to do.' Henry smiled past him.

'I have in fact finished but . . .'

'Good. Go away then.'

The doctor hummed and hawed before finally giving in.

'All right,' he conceded, 'but don't be too long. And don't tire him out.'

'Tire him out? He's been asleep for three days.'

We were left alone and Henry perched on the edge of the bed.

'Well, boy, how are you feeling?'

'It hurts . . .' I whined.

'It's meant to hurt. Being run over by large motor vehicles is supposed to hurt as an incentive to not doing it again. It's Nature's way of telling you that you've been an idiot.'

'I'm sorry, but . . .'

'Yes, I know. That cretin of a driver was more at fault. Anyway, he has been suitably dealt with.'

'Good.' There was a short pause. 'Then what happened?'

'The ambulance arrived, then brought you here and . . .'

'I mean in the court.'

'Oh, that.' Henry went very quiet.

'Yes?' I prompted.

'Well,' he began, 'it was all a bit messy. I asked for the whole thing to be postponed indefinitely but Murchie and co. insisted that it was a matter of the utmost urgency. In the end we just waited to see if there was enough of you left to be worth arguing over and, once it was clear you were safely across the road to recovery, carried on as planned after a few days adjournment.'

'But what happened then?'

'Well, I did try,' he said ruefully.

'And?'

'I tried my best to get rid of you. They asked if I had neglected

173

you. "Neglected!" I cried. "I have positively abused him. He has been starved, half-drowned, left to die of exposure in the hills, subjected to the vilest mental torture and last, but by no means least, thrown under a car." It was all going quite splendidly until he turned up and ruined it.'

'Who's he?'

'MacIntyre. Who else? Came in with his big reliable country doctor routine – "I have visited the house on many occasions and spoken to the boy in private blah blah, can vouch for his complete physical and mental welfare etc etc." Murchie whined a bit about your spiritual well being in that oily way of his, but he and his cronies only succeeded in making complete fools of themselves. Hardly surprising. It became quite amusing at that point. Their argument was almost a work of art in its perfect lack of any sense or logic. Having decided that I had corrupted and intimidated you, they supported this claim with the evidence that you had said, and also written in a letter, that you were perfectly happy. Brilliant, eh? This they said was perfect proof of my bad influence, as no child could truly be happy living with such as me.' He cackled darkly to emphasise this point. 'However, it all back fired somewhat. Do you remember writing a letter to that awful Calder woman?'

'Aunt Margaret? Yes, I do.'

'Well, their *pièce de résistance* was that very letter, written, they argued, under extreme duress and posted in my presence, thus proving that you were being forced to feign happiness. All splendid stuff, but not as good as the outcome. Not only was this "evidence" thrown out of court, but those concerned found themselves in rather hot water for interfering with the Royal Mail. I think that the wretched Graham is going to be in serious trouble with the Post Office. May even lose his position with a bit of luck.' Henry stopped speaking and smiled in a satisfied manner.

This was all very well. I now knew what had happened to everyone except . . .

'But what about me? What's going to happen?'

Henry sighed. 'Well, as I said, I did try my best but . . .'

'But what?' My agitation was making my head hurt.

'But,' he said sadly, 'I'm afraid I'm stuck with you.'

thirty-one

In which we come across an old friend

It was to be another week before I could go home. I grew rather bored lying around in bed, usually by myself although Henry did visit regularly bringing supplies of books and fruit. I was more than relieved when the tubes were removed and was soon able to get up and about, stretching stiff and aching muscles.

Henry arrived early on the last day. He brought with him a bag of clean clothes for me. After breakfast we said our goodbyes to the hospital staff and thanked them for all their help. I was surprised at just how charming Henry could be when he put his mind to it, although the strain was beginning to show by the time we left. A taxi took us to the station, through streets still bristling in the ominous heat. We even passed the fateful crossing and a chill ran through my guts as well as a mild feeling of disappointment at the way it looked so ordinary. Still, what was I expecting? A plaque?

Henry helped me onto the train and we settled down by the window in an almost empty carriage. We were both watching people come and go on the platform and listening to the gulls squabbling above when the train began to move. Someone had been saying copious goodbyes through the window of the door and now sat themselves down in the seat across the aisle from us. I glanced round casually then span my still fragile head back to the window far faster than I should have done.

'Henry!' I whispered. He didn't hear. 'Henry!' it squeaked out.

'Yes?' He looked round. I gave a series of frantic sideways nods with my head.

'Something wrong with your neck?'

'No,' I continued my stage whisper. 'Over there.' I pointed as subtly as I could manage.

Henry looked round with calm indifference. Then one of those smiles crept across his face as his gaze was met by the glazed stare of a moth-eaten head. It was her! Fox-stole was on her way home. Henry looked back at me and raised an eyebrow. I had to try very hard not to giggle. We both sat with our faces glued to the window, showing an almost fanatical interest in the passing scenery. The trembling muscles in my face were verging on the uncontrollable when a genteel throat-clearing broke the silence. We ignored it. And the second, louder 'ahem'. It was only when a voice said 'Excuse me?' that we turned round.

'I'm sorry to trouble you, but haven't I seen you somewhere before?'

'I doubt it, madam,' said Henry and we both shook our heads furiously.

'You do look awfully familiar . . .' We knew that the truth would have to dawn eventually. It did.

'I know. On the way up here. I'm afraid that I was rather rude to you. I really must apologise. I had had such an awful day and I must have been feeling rather harassed. I do apologise. I didn't realise at the time that . . .'

'That's quite all right madam. We all make mistakes.' Henry smiled graciously before turning back to me and raising an eyebrow again so that my sides contracted even further.

How different this journey was. Henry no longer seemed like the most evil man in the world. The court threat no longer hung over my head. It was another glorious day and I watched the hills pass with relish. Communications with fox-stole were kept on the level of polite nods and smiles whenever she happened to catch our eye.

All was well until our stop approached. Then history began to repeat itself.

'Give me your hand, boy.' Henry pulled me up out of my seat, then he himself stood up. We shuffled over to the door. The train creaked to a halt, the door was opened and, with Henry's help, I lowered myself carefully onto the platform, which was, of course, on fox-stole's side of the train. She smiled discreetly through the window as we began to walk. Henry, so as not to lose me, had to slow down his usual striding pace but still ambled up the platform looking the picture of health. Meanwhile, I followed slowly with one painful dead weight of a leg trailing behind me. It all took a moment to register on her face, but the blank expression was soon filled in as the wrinkles of confusion blackened into knitted brows, the window almost steaming up with wordless exasperation. Henry took one look at my snail's pace progress, then at the face behind the glass, before crying 'A camera, a camera, my kingdom for a camera.'

However, before the scene had any chance of being recorded for posterity the train had hauled away the goldfish mouthings, sparing us the possible sight of over-pressurised blood vessels which might, at any moment, explode – like our laughter, which sent the pigeons rattling off down the track.

It was the wrong time of day for the irregular bus service so I sat on a wall outside the station while Henry went to phone for a taxi. We waited for a while in the sun.

'How are you feeling?' he asked.

'A lot better, though this leg still hurts.'

'Don't worry we'll soon have you fed and rested and before you know it you'll be rampaging round the countryside on that bicycle again . . . ah, here we are.'

The taxi drew up and I fitted myself into the back seat. It was a quiet journey. The driver said nothing, probably feeling it his duty to maintain the traditions of the bus in its absence. We were nearly in the village when Henry suddenly spoke.

'Could you turn into the High Street, please? I need one or two things from the shop.'

We stopped by the shop window.

'I won't be long,' said Henry as he climbed out. The door of the shop closed behind him and I could hear the silence oozing out onto the pavement, pervading the whole street. After the court business the odd goings-on of my last visit to the shop now made a lot more sense. All that secret stuff with the letter. That's what they were up to. But then, that means that the letter never got to Aunt Margaret. Maybe I should try again. I waited. Henry seemed to be taking his time. The sullen driver drummed his fingers on the steering-wheel. I began to grow a bit worried. If Henry had gone to rub salt into the wound of his vanquished attackers, then they might not take it too kindly. To say the least. As more time passed I decided to follow him, on the pretext of wanting to buy some stamps. I climbed out of the door with some difficulty and hobbled into the shop. Henry was just being served when the door closed behind me. A host of angry faces stared at me. Even Henry turned round, as if worried that someone was managing to upstage his famous shop-silencing act.

'Hello!' He called cheerfully. This went down like a dirty joke at a cremation. I smiled and looked around nervously. 'I won't be long,' he continued, 'anything that you need?'

'Well, I did want a couple of stamps . . .' I replied. Very quietly.

'Stamps eh? Hmm, I'm not sure about that. Are you still allowed to sell stamps, Graham?' This didn't go down terribly well either. But the stamps were bought all the same. My sweaty fingers stuck to the gum as we turned to leave, Henry smiling gleefully at the wall of dismal faces. An aggressive-looking youth, with short dyed hair and a certain economy of forehead stood in our way. I think he was one of the Graham family. Henry looked down his nose at him and smiled.

'I do so admire such individualism,' he said. 'How very courageous of you to stand so firmly while everyone else gave in to the tide of evolution. Well done.' The youth, despite the absence of a translator, seemed to sense that he had just been insulted, for his lip curled a little. Henry remained quite unperturbed and smiled again. He leaned over and spoke into the youth's face. His words were quiet and intoned with great care.

'You,' he said, 'are in my way.' The proximity of the Dundas countenance seemed to have the desired effect, for he moved with the turn of Henry's head, as if pinned at the end of his gaze.

'Good boy,' was his reward. 'Now why don't you run along and try to become extinct?'

The taxi driver muttered mutinously all the way up the hill, straightening his miserable face only slightly when we piled out in front of the house and Henry told him to keep the change. He mumbled some perfunctory thanks, then turned off back down the hill. We stood for a moment between the holly trees.

'Well, here we are again,' said Henry, then, adopting the persona of some evil P.O.W. camp commandant, declared – 'You will have realised by now that there is no escape. Nothing can save you. The hills, the law, even death itself – all useless. You might as well accept it. Besides, it's time for lunch.'

After lunch I went into solitary confinement for a while, resting in my room. Before lying down I wrote another letter to Aunt Margaret. This was a very different letter from its predecessor. None of the truth was disguised. I was happy here, and I stated this with a defiance which embossed itself on several sheets below. In the interests of dignity I left out some of the more onomatopaeic expressions which ran through my mind, and instead saved them as an accompaniment to the thump of my fist that sealed the envelope.

Having stated my case so firmly I settled down on the bed with a book. I had endured more than enough bedridden days, but this was different. This felt like home. I must have dozed off for a while, because I came round with a start, wondering for a moment where I was. Henry had come in to the room.

'All right?' he asked.

'Yes. I just nodded off for a bit.'

'Sorry to disturb you, but I forgot about this.'

He held up a paper bag. 'My purchase from Graham's shop.' He tossed it onto the bed. I opened the bag to find two large bars of chocolate, the same kind that had once dissolved in the rain of my abortive escape attempt. My eyes lit up after so much hospital food.

'But don't spoil your appetite,' Henry warned. 'Supper will be at the usual hour.'

'Thank you,' I murmured shyly.

'See you later. And no charging up and down the stairs,' he said, nodding earnestly towards my leaden leg.

The leg and I stayed pretty much where we were for the rest of the afternoon. It was a great relief to have a bit of privacy once more, no doctors and nurses shuttling in and out of the room to prod and pester. I read some more and kept myself amused until supper time.

Supper was a pleasant if not entirely memorable affair. Henry spent a great deal of time doing his best to make me laugh so that my numerous tender parts ached all the more, but it was not this that stuck in my mind. Once the meal was over Henry suggested that an early night was in order.

'I don't know about you but I feel worn out. You look pretty tired too.'

'Yes, I do feel very tired,' I admitted. We walked down the hall, stopping outside the study door.

'You can manage the stairs all right?'

'I think so thanks,' I replied, beginning to climb.

'Jolly good. Sleep well and I'll see you in the morning.'

'Right. Goodnight, Henry.'

'Goodnight, Roderick.'

thirty-two

❦

Days in the garden

There was one thing to be said for the hospital. No boiler. But familiarity breeds content and even this dawn intrusion seemed quite homely. It rumbled and gurgled its welcome as I stretched and wondered what to do with the day.

The state of my leg was far more effective in curtailing my wanderings than even the manacles in the shed might have been. However, I had spent quite enough time indoors, so the only remaining possibility was the garden and it was there that I was to spend the majority of my time. Henry produced, from some dark corner of the shed, a pair of deck-chairs, their striped canvas a little faded but still reasonably secure. I tackled them in the traditional manner, arranging the small number of moving parts in the almost infinite number of permutations which they seemed to allow. Observing my plight Henry smiled and came striding over from his vegetable watering with an air of determined competence.

'Give it to me,' he cried laughingly, then proceeded to embarrass himself by repeating, move for move, my own performance.

'If you hadn't felt it necessary to rearrange your anatomy like that you could have just sat on the grass like a normal boy,' he protested, trapping his finger. Eventually, after much cursing, and not a little giggling, one of nature's greatest secrets was revealed to us and the writhing mass of wood and canvas congealed into something not unlike a chair. Exhausted we collapsed into the seats, which sagged alarmingly but resisted the temptation to wring any further slapstick from the situation.

'It wasn't easy,' Henry declared earnestly, 'but I knew we could do it.' We leaned over for a celebratory hand shake.

When he wasn't busying himself about the garden Henry would join me in the neighbouring deck-chair. The chairs remained firmly planted by the side of the lawn, under the shade of the oaks. They were even left there overnight, as we had decided that the risk of rain was nothing compared to the thought of another titanic struggle. Here we would sit, Henry accompanied by a sizeable chunk of his library which would steadily migrate out onto the lawn during the course of the day. Every so often he would pad thoughtfully into the house, always returning with another volume to which he would refer, then add it to the pile. By the end of the afternoon he would have amassed such a heap of books that it took several trips to return them all to the study.

Even in the shade I still found myself prone to headaches, an after-effect of my accident of which I had been forewarned when I left the hospital. On the occasions when these attacks did overtake me I found it impossible to read and was forced to sit back with my eyes shut. Henry was not unsympathetic. He would fetch me glasses of water and, during one bout, declared that he knew of just the thing to cheer me up. He disappeared into the house, emerging after a while with another addition to the book mountain. This particular volume was opened on his lap and, with a clearing of his throat, he began to read.

The story concerned three men in a boat, a title which at first failed to show a great deal of promise as far as I was concerned. My mind was soon changed as there unfolded a tale of human foibles which made even our deck-chair raising seem quite respectable. Nor was it just the humour of the story itself which delighted me. Even more amusing was the sight of Henry struggling through his favourite passages with tears rolling down his cheeks, desperately trying to regain his breath as the words vanished helplessly into the laughing depths of his beard. At times his whole long frame would slither down the chair until his knees stuck up towards the sun and he would lie trembling with silent laughter. Much though I enjoyed the story it was this sight that cheered me most, infectiously reducing me to a similar state which did little for my headaches but much for my heart.

When we were exhausted by our giggling, or just bedrowsed by the lazy hum of the summer, we would doze off, swatting sleepily at flies, or just lie back and watch the few white clouds sail past, high and far away from our own little world.

Unfortunately, the large, clumsy world was intent on intruding. It did so during a giggling session. A car pulled up outside the house and a hand knocked firmly at the door. Henry, having just completed one of his slithers, did not have the energy, or inclination, to move, so called out instead.

'We're in the garden.'

His voice must have carried, for footsteps sounded on the gravel and round the corner of the house appeared a police officer.

'Oh dear,' said Henry, 'he must have come to arrest you for reckless walking.'

'Sorry to disturb you, sir . . .'

'Well don't then,' Henry replied.

'But I'm afraid I must. We're distributing these.'

He handed a pamphlet to Henry.

'It's fairly self-explanatory. Sorry to disturb you.'

He sounded genuinely apologetic and left quickly.

Henry began to read through the pamphlet. Then he began to laugh.

'What is it?' I asked.

'This,' he snorted, 'is a leaflet telling us just how easy it is to protect oneself against nuclear attack by using only the simplest of household furniture and utensils.' He continued to laugh but stopped when another car sounded outside.

'Who is it now?' he muttered impatiently.

This time it was MacIntyre who came striding rotundly round the house.

'Good day to you, Henry,' he cried in a cheerful manner which was no doubt calculated to annoy.

'Oh Lord. This is all we need. That is one of the worst side effects of road accidents. They tend to attract the medical profession.'

'I just thought I would call round and see how you were doing.'

'I'm fine thank you,' Henry said. 'Goodbye.'

'Not you, you old fool. How's young Roderick?'

'I'm all right, thanks, although my leg's still sore and I keep getting these headaches.'

'Aye, but I'm afraid that's only to be expected. It will be a wee while yet before you're back to normal.'

'That is,' Henry interrupted, 'if we have a wee while left.' He waved his pamphlet.

'Oh, you've got your magic leaflet, have you? Marvellous isn't it? It quite surprised me. Over thirty years in the medical profession and I hadn't realised that it was physically possible to write with your head up your bum.' He laughed one of his raucous laughs before continuing. 'Mind you, it's not a patch on the one I got a few weeks ago, and I quote, "In the event of a nuclear attack, access to some medical supplies and facilities may be disrupted." A reasonable assumption, don't you think?'

Henry nodded earnestly before joining the laughter. I didn't find it quite so funny.

'Is there really going to be a war?'

'Who knows?' MacIntyre answered more seriously. 'But I'll tell you one thing. If it does happen I'm damned if I'm going to chase around like a blue-arsed fly clearing up the mess. There's enough in my medicine cabinet to see me safely out of the way. And a select few of my patients should they require a prescription.'

He winked at Henry, who sat back in his chair.

'Don't worry about us, MacIntyre. We'll have a splendid view from up here. Wouldn't want to miss that, would we?'

I was quite happy to miss it. And I had a feeling that even Henry's enthusiasm had waned a little, although, to keep up appearances it was still necessary to talk that way. Whatever the reason, I wished that he wouldn't. I didn't want a war. Not now anyway. It was coming at the wrong time. It should have been weeks ago when, with my world in tatters, I didn't care what happened. But now I had too much to lose. Still, if they absolutely insisted then I would just have to put up with it. In which case, the first day of the new school term would be as good a time as any.

On the other hand, why worry about the mere end of the world? After all, far worse things could happen. And they did.

thirty-three

The tale of a brother

It had been transparently clear from the start that my welfare played, at most, a very minor role in the motives of those who had brought the court case which was to rescue me from Henry's clutches. Their intention was not to help me but to hurt Henry, not so much by taking me away, the effect of which was an unknown quantity to them and me, but by having some official stamp of approval placed on their petty fears and hatred. If it could be shown in a court that Henry had gone too far, if he was to be shown to be more than just their personal bugbear, then they would be satisfied. They needed to be assured that this man really was evil, even by the standards of the outside world. Had they succeeded I doubt if any of it would have bothered Henry. No matter how grand or official any opinion of him could be, he would still have regarded it with amused contempt. The court's condemnation would have meant nothing to him. Just how he would have been troubled by the loss of me . . . Well, I still didn't like to think about that too much. Especially not now that it was an academic question. The whole attack on Henry had been doomed from the start. Win or lose the case, they could only lose the battle. You can only win at a game if the other person plays by the same set of rules. So, not only had they failed, they had humiliated themselves in the process. I had witnessed none of the events in court, but could well imagine how Henry would have behaved. When it suited him he could present himself with a charm and eloquence which would soon have knocked the stuffing out of Murchie and co's evidence. What's more, the official disapproval which they had sought like bullied children had all fallen on them, and they were beginning to suffer for it. All this meant that they had all the more reason for wanting to get at Henry. And in this frightened and angry world they found a way, a way that was far more effective than any court could have been.

I will always remember those days in the garden as one of the most peaceful and civilised times of my life. We floated on a little island above the snowballing barbarities of the world outside. The worse it grew out there, the more we enjoyed ourselves in the warm peace of the garden. Henry had even taken to ignoring his radio, taking little interest in the insistent hissing of the fuse that sounded low behind the euphemisms of the news readers. We seemed safely sealed off from that world, and indeed we were. However, whatever magic it was that protected us in the garden was to vanish as soon as someone stepped outside.

The spell first began to waver when I woke one morning to the sound of silence. At first I thought I was back in the hospital, that it had all been a dream, but I wakened slowly to the realisation that the pattern had been broken. This was something I had quite forgotten about. This was a disappearing day. It was a disappearing day like any of the others that had gone before, except in one very peculiar respect. Something I could never have imagined happening to me went ahead and happened. I missed Henry. I actually missed having him around. The deck-chairs were there, Oscar was there, a plate of sandwiches, everything about the garden was the same but for one thing. No Henry. The atmosphere just wasn't the same. Still, it was only one day, so I resigned myself to temporary solitude, opened a book and settled back in the sun to wait.

I didn't have to wait very long. I was half dozing in the deck-chair when I started to the sound of what I thought was a door slamming. I listened carefully, but could hear nothing else. My curiosity was aroused so I began to walk slowly back to the house.

186

Inside it seemed unnaturally dark as my eyes adjusted to the gloom of the shade. I stopped in the kitchen and listened again. The tap dripped very slightly. I could hear my heart beating, but nothing else. But then, a faint bump, coming from the study. It could have been burglars. It could have been the enraged villagers coming to exact revenge. It could have been all manner of things of that kind, but my usually fevered imagination didn't even bother to list them. There was no need to reach for bread knives or blunt instruments. Some sixth sense, probably awakened by the blow to my head, told me that this was not something to be afraid of, at least, not in that way. I walked slowly down the hall and stopped outside the study. I knocked on the door. No reply, although I knew that there was someone in there. I knocked again and waited, then turned the handle slowly. No one jumped on me as I entered, certainly not Henry, who sat, bolt upright on the settee, staring into the space between him and the bookshelves.

'Henry?' He didn't respond. 'Henry?' I moved round into his line of sight, but it still didn't seem to register. His eyes kept staring blankly, quite motionless until, very slowly, a solitary tear began to course jerkily down his cheek. In the interests of symmetry his other eye responded, and two tears settled in his beard like dew.

'Henry? What's the matter?' He continued to stare, his eyes wet and helpless. I waited so long that I almost jumped when at last he did speak.

'The stone. Robert's stone. They've broken Robert's stone.' He spoke slowly, with an air of complete disbelief. 'It's broken. With a hammer, a rock, I don't know.' Then his head sank into his hands and stayed there.

I grew nervous. When Henry was being frightening that was one thing. But this was terrifying.

'What do you mean?' I asked. 'Who's Robert?'

Henry said nothing, but sank back on the settee and lay there with his hands covering his face.

'Henry?' I didn't know what to do. 'I . . . well . . . Would you like some tea?'

He nodded very slowly from behind his hands, so I hobbled off to the kitchen in as much of a rush as I could manage and put the kettle on.

When I came back to the study Henry had re-arranged himself on the settee and now lay in his Egyptian sarcophagus position. I handed him the tea and he sipped slowly before putting the cup down on the table. I sat down and waited, unable to think of anything else to do or say.

'Sorry about this,' he said at last, rubbing at his eyes. 'I've had a bit of a shock.'

'Where have you been?'

'Where I always go when I disappear. To Robert's grave.'

There was another long pause. I waited for him to elaborate, but my patience soon ran out.

'Who was Robert?'

Henry sighed, re-arranged himself a bit more, then drank some more tea. He shook his head slowly then began to speak.

'Robert was my brother. My older brother. Maybe I haven't mentioned him before, but I think I once did, when we were repairing the bicycle. He always used to sort me out when I did stupid things – like taking tyres off with screw drivers.'

I remembered the reference and nodded.

'We were in a similar position to yourself. Being a traditionally short-lived family, our father died when we were both very young. Mother waited around a bit longer, and then passed away when she felt that Robert was old enough to put up with looking after me. We were surprisingly close for siblings and he did look after me very well. Oh, we fought of course as all brothers do, but most of the time it was all right, and he took care of me. At least, until I was old enough to fend for myself, when he went away.' Henry drank some more tea then looked round at me. 'I'm not boring you, am I?'

'No, no, not at all.' I shook my head vigorously, busily trying to visualise a small Henry, with some difficulty.

'He was a very idealistic sort was Robert. He and your Father would have got on well had they ever met. Robert took a more fashionable path to saving the world. He went off to the Poet's War, in Spain, to drive back the fascist beast before it overran the world. He wasn't there for long. He came back, almost in tears, saying that he couldn't bear the sight of anyone else's life flashing before his eyes. I was a bit disappointed, being caught up in the long-range romance of the thing. "Who's winning?" I asked. "No one," he said.

He said that victory was a self-contradictory idea – it couldn't exist without defeat, and so was never more than half the story – always less than the truth. Unfortunately, the war business was catching. Soon everyone was at it. I was too young to be involved but Robert wasn't. The King wrote to him asking for the pleasure of his company at one end or the other of a bayonet. Robert wrote back and told him to stick his offer where royalty meets the throne. Of course, he had a lot of trouble convincing them that he was a genuine conscientious objector. It's rather a hard case to pass off when you've just spent several months taking pot shots at Spanish fascists of your own accord. They wouldn't accept his arguments and he wouldn't wear their uniform. So they compromised and threw him in gaol. He spent his time sewing mail bags for the war effort. One day a bomb fell outside the prison. A piece of shrapnel came through the window of the cell and imbedded itself in the wall just above his bunk. He said that if he hadn't been using the bucket in the corner at the time he wouldn't have lived to tell the tale. It would have been a marvellously ironic death, one which the propagandists would have relished. "We must fight to ensure that our prisoners can sleep safely in their cells." They let him out eventually, once Japan had surrendered after a bit of experimental persuasion. He left with enough white feathers stuck to his records to make a sizeable eiderdown. Not that he cared. He still didn't think that anyone had won. He certainly hadn't. The war caught up with him in the end. The shrapnel was just the start of the joke. The punch line was still to come.'

Henry stopped and reached for his tea. 'I'm sure you've had enough old history for today. It's all in the past. After all, we've a war of our own to look forward to.'

'What happened to him?'

'Well, he came back home. I suppose it was all my fault really. I suggested a celebration, I'd cooked quite a splendid meal with the rations I had been saving, and we went to get something to drink. Nothing grand, just a few bottles of beer from the pub. That was where we made the mistake. If you think that the silences I produce are impressive, you should have heard this one. Every face in that bar turned round and every eye tried to burn through us. Robert was used to it, but I was furious, and a bit scared. He just asked

189

politely for what he wanted while I glared back at them all. 'We don't serve traitors in here,' said the landlord. I remember almost lunging forward, but Robert steadied me and just smiled. 'Come on Henry, let's away and have this supper of yours.' There was someone barring the door, a big, ugly oaf who wore a lost finger as a red badge of courage. 'And we don't want any traitors in this village,' he said, but with a few colourful adjectives of his own. Then the others joined in. They were bored with peace already. They started to push Robert around, but he just ignored them and waited for a chance to leave. I stepped in and it was when someone knocked me aside that Robert first reacted. We're not a small family and I don't think he knew what had hit him. It was an upper-cut of some grace and power that laid him out. That quietened them for a bit, but the "traitor" motif re-asserted itself. They went for both of us. The Dundas's had gone to war at last. And we gave them some stick. There are still a few misshapen old noses in that village that I can proudly claim as mine. When the landlord saw that the "traitors" were doing rather well he 'phoned for the police. I think he was worried about his windows. It was then that we found out who the real cowards were. Someone pulled a knife. We didn't see it, didn't know anything about it until Robert fell, clutching his side. There was blood coming out of his mouth. "Not bad for a pacifist, eh Henry?" I remember he smiled as he said it. It was the last thing he ever did. The whole room fell silent. I stared around, then saw the knife, in the hand, with the sheet white face above it. I screamed and roared so loud that every face in the room turned the same colour. I hit him with my whole body. I don't remember crossing the room. I just flew across it. All I remember is sitting over his chest, with the knife in my hand, Robert's blood dripping onto his white collar. I pressed the knife against his throat. And do you know what I did?'

Henry paused.

'Nothing. I did absolutely nothing. Nobody even hauled me off. I just stood up and walked away. I remember carrying Robert out into the street, then collapsing onto my knees with the weight of him. I tried to bawl that village to the ground. I howled and swore till every light went on, every curtain twitched open. That's all I remember. That and the funeral. Not in the village of course. They wouldn't sully their holy earth with the carcass of a traitor. No, it was held outside the glen, on the way to Inverness. That's where I go, to keep it tidy, take fresh flowers from the garden. But now . . . NOW!' he shouted, 'now they have broken his stone. And it's my fault again. I got him into the fight. I stirred them up again. It's always the same.' The tears began to roll again. This great mass of a man, this breaker of noses and silencer of whole villages, was crying like a child. I half knelt before him, clumsy with my stiff leg, and reached out a hand, nervous and confused.

'Henry? I . . .'

He spoke almost angrily. 'I know what you're thinking. Old Henry has a grudge. His secret is out. All this metaphysical misanthropy is plain nonsense, he just has one almighty grudge. Well, you're wrong. I wish that was all that it was, but it's far, far worse. It's not me, it's the whole halfway world. But this time there won't be any problem. This time the war will come out as it should. There won't be any victory. Not of any kind for anyone. Redemption cometh at last. What did I do that night? What did I do? Nothing. Absolutely nothing. I could have killed him. I could have killed him as easily as that. It was no more than he deserved. But I didn't. I walked away. But only halfway, always half of the way. I didn't kill, but I never, ever forgave. I will not and cannot forgive. That's what's wrong with twisted old Henry. He's the epitome of this whole damned world. Always halfway.'

He stopped and seemed to calm down a little.

'I,' he said at last, 'am one of the eternal losers. Too strong to fight, but far too weak to surrender. The war is inside us all. But this time there will be no half measures.'

thirty-four

In which the end is even more nigh than usual

Time was slipping away fast. And so was Henry. A black cloud hung over him so plainly that, given one quick draught of cool air, it would start to rain on his head, even under the ceiling of the study where he now spent the vast majority of his time, emerging only to half eat his meals if he ate at all. Life at Halfway House seemed to have gone full circle, back to the days when meal times were silent, the house silent, dark and frightening and when Henry fully lived up to his reputation as world's greatest misanthrope. I did little to break this silence, not because I was afraid, but because I could think of nothing to say. I remember one short exchange over supper.

'Henry?'

'Yes?' He didn't look up.

'Is there anything I can do?'

He paused for a while before looking up with the very faintest of smiles.

'Yes,' he said. 'Just keep me away from trees.'

There was no need to keep him away from anything. He remained firmly ensconced in the study, emerging less and less, neglecting his meals and even the usually regular baths. Had he not already been in possession of a large beard I'm sure he would have stopped shaving as well.

It was worrying to waken each morning to a dormant boiler. Every day I would panic, fearing that Henry had gone off to complete some dark unfinished business, but every morning I would find him in the study, sitting quietly at his desk. I would make tea and toast, then take it in to him, hoping that he would at least eat something. Henry would smile and quietly thank me before telling me to run along and enjoy the sun while I could.

'Go on. Make the most of it. There isn't much time.'

He was right. There wasn't much time.

The morning which had been set aside for the end of the world was close and sticky. One look out of the window revealed a deep grey sky and the air was thick and hot. Perhaps it was the stifling, thundery heat that did it, but, on that one morning, Henry did decide to have a bath. Perhaps it was some instinct that told him, a variation on the wearing of clean underwear in case of road accidents. Whatever the reason, I was wakened by a familiar cacophony, the horrendous glurpings of my old friend the boiler. This cheered me up a bit, especially when I noticed that it was still quite early. I could have gone back to sleep, but my stomach vetoed this idea so I hauled myself out from beneath the covers, pulled on my dressing-gown and headed for the kitchen. I found Henry there, making tea.

'Good morning,' he said in a subdued voice, 'you're up early.'

'I felt hungry,' I replied.

'Well, there's plenty of bread for toast. Help yourself.' He wandered off towards the study.

'I'm just going to listen to the news on the wireless, then I'll have my bath.'

The door closed and I set about slicing the loaf. I made quite a good job of it by my standards, lit the grill and waited for it to heat up a bit. It was then, as I waited, that another sound began to rise above the roar of the gas. It drifted in through the open window, distant and muffled by the thick air. A bell was ringing. The church bell. But this wasn't Sunday . . . Then a laugh that was almost a cheer. The door flew open and there stood Henry, grinning from ear to ear.

'They've done it!' He announced.

'Who's done it? And what have they done?'

'They've pressed the button at last.'

'The button?'

'The war. They've started the war.'

'But, but . . . when? How? NOW?'

'Yes, now. I think four minutes is the estimated time of arrival.' He glanced over at the grill. 'So I hope you don't like your toast well done!'

'But Henry! Where are you going?'

'Upstairs. To watch, of course.' He bounded up the stairs and left me alone with two slices of bread and a war to cope with. I was too astonished to panic, I just stood gawping for a while and turning around in a particularly unconstructive fashion. I looked out of the window. There, on the coal bunker, lay Oscar, completely unperturbed by the whole affair. He stretched lazily, dangling his tail over the edge, then fell fast asleep. Why am I watching the cat? I'm going to die. Protect yourself, quickly. I would need food. I had bread, so I grabbed the rest of the loaf and a tin of tomatoes before fleeing into the hall. The cupboard under the stairs! That would be the place. The door was stiff and I tugged and yanked until it gave suddenly, sending me tumbling backwards. I scrambled inside, pulling the door shut as best I could without trapping my fingers. Well, all right, I did trap my fingers, but there was more at stake. Then I waited. It was very dark under the stairs. It smelled musty and faintly of polish. My leg was wrapped awkwardly round the vacuum cleaner. In one corner the electricity meter ticked ominously. I could sense a thousand spiders queueing up to dive down my collar. I waited some more. No sound but that steady ticking. Should I eat some bread now or wait until later? How long would I have to hide? Still I waited. I needed to go to the toilet. I put the tin down on something that felt cold and squashy and didn't dare pick it up again. Besides, I had forgotten the tin opener. And still I waited.

194

I have no idea just how long it was before I heard the explosion, but I'm pretty sure that I sat in that thick darkness for a lot longer than four minutes. It sounded a long way off, muffled and dull. Then silence. I braced myself, closed my eyes and waited. The spiders had paled into insignificance. Well, almost. Any minute now it would come, the great wind, the waves of death sweeping across the hills, rocking the whole house. Here they come, yes . . . no, not quite. I began to untense a little as fear gave way to cramp. The winds and waves of death were certainly taking their time. I gave them a fairly generous allowance of meter ticks before growing impatient. What's happening? I could wait no longer. Perhaps if I made it to Henry's wireless I could find out what was going on. I gave it a couple more minutes, in which only silence disturbed the house, then very cautiously began to open the door. Or, rather, try to open the door. I was suddenly seized by the terrible thought that in the middle of a false alarm I was about to suffocate to death in a cupboard full of spiders. I gave one almighty shove and tumbled out into the hall in a tangle of vacuum cleaner and squashed loaf.

'Oh my God! What are you doing here?' cried a familiar figure in a neat green suit, recoiling in obvious horror as I shot out near his feet.

'I live here,' I protested. 'Although I suppose "live" isn't really the word any more.'

'What do you mean?'

'Well, the war of course. You must have come to . . .'

'Certainly not,' he snapped. 'I do not intend going through all that business again. Not with you. Not for a long, long time if I can help it.'

'Oh.' I felt vaguely insulted by this. 'But what about . . . I mean, I thought that they had pressed the button?'

'Yes, they did,' he said in a very matter of fact way.

'And?'

'And what?'

'And what happened?' I asked greedily, standing up and dusting myself off.

'Nothing.' He replied calmly. 'Absolutely nothing.'

'But, I thought that . . .'

'I don't care what you thought. The fact is that we have decided against it. The war has been cancelled.'

'Cancelled?' I was a mite confused.

'Yes, that is what I said, cancelled, as in called off. I'm afraid you still have far too much to learn, too much to get sorted out. What muddled little creatures you are. The only animal that prays and plans before ripping out throats. Well, we've decided that it's about time that you made up your minds just what you are going to be – one thing or t'other. In the meantime, don't think that there's an easy way out. You will just have to wait until you learn.' He turned to go, but added, 'Besides, think of the administrative problems it would have caused for me. Goodbye.'

I called after him. 'But wait a minute. If there hasn't been a war, then what are you doing . . .?'

'I won't tell you again, child. You delayed me more than enough the last time.'

'Sorry,' I answered with a certain sarcasm.

'Although,' he looked back and smiled, 'despite the nature of our work, we're not entirely without a sense of humour.'

The door closed behind him. I stood looking bemused, mostly at the way that someone in his position still used doors. But never mind that. The world was saved. And what's more, I hadn't done anything embarrassing while I waited for it to end. Mind you, I had squashed the loaf a bit. I tried to knead it back into shape but soon abandoned that task and hobbled up the stairs to break the news to Henry. I hoped that he wouldn't be too disappointed.

He was in my room, I could tell by the way the door was ajar. I found him sitting at the desk, looking out across the valley.

'Henry,' I cried, 'you'll never guess what's happened.' He didn't reply as I walked up behind him.

'Henry?' I tapped his arm. His hand slid from the desk and onto his lap. 'Henry?' I grew afraid. His eyes were closed and across his face there rested the most serene of smiles. He was quite dead.

I didn't understand. What had happened? I span around, as if some explanation would kindly stand up and present itself from some corner of the room. Oddly enough, it did. From beneath the

196

wardrobe a pool of water was beginning to form, steaming slightly on the floor. Of course. The boiler. We had forgotten all about the boiler. The bang that I heard. Henry's heart. It all made sense. Henry had gone down with his plumbing. Not that he knew that, and, even though I knew that he was dead, I didn't have the heart to tell him. For him the world had ended. He was no longer a prisoner of memory, no longer the eternal halfway loser. Redemption had come at last. And did he look happy about it? Yes, he most certainly did. Very happy and extremely pleased with himself. The only man in the world allowed an easy way out.

'Oh Henry,' I muttered, feeling myself begin to cry. But he smiled back most infectiously, so much so that my face became a wrestling match of mixed expressions as a foolish grin rose to meet the tears.

'Oh Henry!' I knelt on the floor beside him.

It was then that I jumped. A bang, a world-shattering roar. He had lied. Who in their right mind would trust him of all people? Rushing to the window and staring out over the garden. The bang turned to a rumble, then an ominous silence. Down below, in the garden, Oscar woke with a start. He jumped down from his bunker, twitched, then shook himself frantically before running for the shelter of the house. It took more than the end of the world to shift him. I smiled and turned back to Henry as, out in the garden, and perhaps across the whole waiting world, the first big drops began to fall.

ROBERT LOUIS STEVENSON 1850 – 1894

RLS: A LIFE STUDY (Jenni Calder)
'In this well-researched and fluently written book
Stevenson emerges as an extraordinary and unusually
gifted Scotsman: delicate, magnanimous, capable of
arousing love in women and devotion in men.'
(Alan Bold, The Scotsman)

'RLS: A LIFE STUDY penetrates the moods and
conflicting desires of a writer who could get and produce
unending excitement from TREASURE ISLAND and, as
well, write masterpieces like THRAWN JANET and
THE MASTER OF BALLANTRAE.'
(Emma Tennant, The Guardian)

ST IVES (R L Stevenson)
This unfinished novel by RLS was written between
January 1893 and October 1894. ST IVES begins in
Edinburgh Castle in 1813, where a French prisoner,
Champdivers (alias St Ives) is being held captive.
A tale of intrigue and suspense unfolds.

Because of RLS's recurrent illnesses this tale was taken
down in dictation by his step-daughter, Bella Strong.
About 6 weeks prior to his death, he laid the story to one
side. Jenni Calder has now, with the prompting of
Bob Storey, written a convincing and colourful new
ending which would have impressed RLS himself.

MEMORIES & PORTRAITS (R L Stevenson)
This book documents aspects of Stevenson's experience of
life and literature, and is full of illumination of his other
works. The essays have a special interest in this wider
context, but they can also be read and enjoyed for their
own sake. They are the product of a meticulous
craftsman, who handled words with scrupulous care, and
wanted to avoid tired images and idea.

NEIL GUNN 1891 — 1973

THE LOST CHART
A cold war thriller set in Glasgow shortly after the Second World War, 'the Lost Chart' moves on two distinct planes — the physical and the metaphysical.

THE LOST GLEN
The famous novel on the decline of Highland ways and values in the 1920s.

THE OTHER LANDSCAPE
Gunn returns to the familiar setting of the Highlands but with a new element of dark humour.

THE SHADOW
A hauntingly beautiful story in which the violence of war and spiritual wastelands are seen through the eyes of a young Scotswoman.

THE SILVER BOUGH
Archaeologist Simon Grant comes to the Highlands to investigate an ancient cairn. A stranger in a strange part of the country, he finds that there are barriers to understanding between him and the people of the community.

SECOND SIGHT
The setting is a Highland shooting lodge, whose occupants are depicted in stark contrast to the local people. A violent death is foreseen. But whose? How? When?

OFF IN A BOAT
The adventures of a man, who at a critical point in his life, throws caution to the wind, and with his wife as Crew, navigates his way round the West Coast of Scotland.

HIGHLAND PACK
This selection of essays follows the pattern imposed on the land by the changing seasons.